MW00440949

Barbados Heat

Also by Don Bruns

Jamaica Blue

Barbados Heat

DON BRUNS

St. Martin's Minotaur ☙ New York

This is a work of fiction. All of the characters and events portrayed in this book are either fictitious or are used fictitiously.

BARBADOS HEAT. Copyright © 2003 by Don Bruns. All rights reserved. Printed in the United States of America. No part of this book may be used or reproduced in any manner whatsoever without written permission except in the case of brief quotations embodied in critical articles or reviews. For information, address St. Martin's Press, 175 Fifth Avenue, New York, N.Y. 10010.

www.minotaurbooks.com

ISBN 0-312-30492-7

First Edition: November 2003

10 9 8 7 6 5 4 3 2 1

To Al and Carol Amero,
the Sarasota connection

Acknowledgments

Frank and Taunia, Randy and Fabiola, thanks for the hospitality. Eric, at Circle Books, it was a great place to start. Dan and Linda, to good drinks and good cigars. Cat, at Fred's, thanks for the Barbados Heat drink recipe. John and Barbara, thanks for taking care of business.

Josh, Charlie, Jane, and Joe, your help was immeasurable.

As always, Sue Grafton, I love you. Thanks for all you've done.

Barbados Heat

Prologue

October 28, 9:30 P.M.

Robert Shapply stepped from the white stretch limo. "That will be all tonight, Charlie."

"Very good, Congressman. I'll pick you up tomorrow at seven A.M." The uniformed chauffeur had been unusually quiet tonight. He closed the door and walked to the driver's side. For just a moment he seemed to stop and survey the area, looking up and down the tree-lined street, then he stepped in and started the car. As he pulled slowly away from the curb, Shapply could hear the increase in the volume of the limo's stereo. The heavy backseat reverberated down the block. The same type of music that the congressman and his wife were working to ban. At one time he'd championed the performers who produced the vile music. Songs about violence, rape, drugs, and whatever else was evil in the world. Now, he was about to bring them down. His transformation would be complete. He had been a *part* of the sin and corruption, the prodigal son. He'd come home to not only make amends but to rid the world of corruption. But there was Barbados.

Only three other people knew about it. Three other people in his life knew and one was threatening to expose him. Possibly it was time to confess it all. Make a tearful, heartfelt confession and throw it on the pile of all his other sins. What was it that his brother-in-law said? The Reverend was fond of saying "Just ask, and he will call a gathering of angels to watch over you." Maybe it was time to ask.

Shapply watched the disappearing automobile, then turned and walked up the brick steps, his hand lightly brushing the ornamental railing that led to his Adams-Morgan townhouse. He stumbled over something, looked down and saw the scuffed boot as it swiftly kicked his feet out from under him. Landing hard on the steps, he struggled to get up and felt the cold steel barrel of a gun pressed against his temple, forcing his head onto the rough bricks. His eyes focused on the boots and a hint of faded blue jeans. The congressman started to speak as the boot swung back and kicked him full force in the face, cracking his expensive capped teeth and catching the end of his nose, snapping the cartilage and plastering it flat against his cheekbone. Blood spurted from his mouth and nose and he fought to catch his breath. Through the agony he found himself thinking only one thought. How could he face the television cameras looking like this? The barrel of the gun pressed harder against his skull and he watched in horror as the boot swung back one more time and drove into his groin. The sharp pain paralyzed him, shooting into all parts of his body as he struggled for consciousness. A wave of nausea overwhelmed him and he vomited, the retching causing even more pain. This time he thought about his life, and wondered if there was forgiveness for unspeakable sins that had never been confessed. Gasping for air, he reached for his crotch as the boot heel stomped on his hand, cracking the bones like toothpicks.

"There has to be some suffering. In just a minute now I'll put you out of your misery." The voice was calm, as if the man were trying to comfort him. Another kick to the stomach, and Shapply vomited all over the boots. "You little fuck!" Now the voice was agitated. "Should have just done this to begin with." That voice. Through the sickness, the pain, and the terror, he recognized the familiar voice. A roar filled his ears for a fraction of a second, then he heard no more.

Chapter One

October 28, 9:30 A.M.

"Shapply? He and his wife are holding some kind of hearings on violence and porn in the entertainment industry, right?" Sever took a small bite of his bagel and washed it down with a swig of black coffee. The Chicago morning was gray and dreary, and rain streaked the windows on his Old Town townhouse. He watched a car go by, tires spitting water in a trail behind.

"It's better than that, dude. This one is right up your alley." The voice on the other end was New York street smart. Jamie Jordan was a young editor who was handling the entertainment division for the daily *New York Hustle*. "Mick, you're gonna love this one. This guy and his wife are getting ready to do Tipper Gore one better. They're gonna have hearings starting next week on lyrics and graphic CD covers. They're not just gonna ask for stronger ratings, they're gonna make every attempt to put a couple of groups, rappers, and labels out of business. I mean permanently."

"Been tried before, Jamie. The musicians and labels always bounce back, bigger and badder than before."

"Yeah, I hear ya, but, Mick, this little campaign has got a ton of money to throw at their project. Her brother, Joseph Evans, he's donating a bunch of money. You know his story?"

"Yeah. Made a reputation doing prison ministries. Turning the rapists and robbers into religious zealots."

"Had a very successful ministry. Very high profile. He helped put Shapply in office. He basically made Shapply a household word. Lately he seems to be relegated to the late-night cable shows, but he still has a strong following and this guy has tons of cash. He's starting a media campaign against rappers and he's gonna sit in on the hearings. Shit, Mick, this story has pizzazz written all over it. You can't afford to turn this down."

Sever was quiet, rolling over the possibilities in his mind. "So her brother, the Reverend Joseph Evans, has the religious right up in arms on this?"

"He does. You remember that thirteen-year-old girl that got raped last month? They've got two guys from Bite Me in jail on that one. And the kid who hung himself while listening to *Suicide Dog*? They've got some serious ammunition."

"Jamie, I really am ready for a break, and sitting around a stuffy hearing somewhere in our nation's capital doesn't exactly excite the hell out of me."

"Mick, you cover the music beat better than anyone. Nobody knows rock and roll like you do. You could write a hell of a series, and name your price. I need a really good kick-ass piece. Rumor has it that you're good friends with Nick Brand, Shapply's stepson. Could be a good angle."

Sever was silent for a moment. He and Nick Brand had been best of friends years ago. They forged a bond stronger than marriage, and they were the kind of friends that nothing came between. Nothing. But something had. And he'd learned a lot about relationships that day. They'd had a major falling out and the chance of ever being friendly with Nick Brand again was hard to imagine. But that wasn't the only reason he didn't want the job. He'd just come off his book tour for *Jamaica Blue*, the story of Derrick and the Laments and the string of murders that followed the band. He was tired, strung out, and he really didn't need another gig right now. Hell, he didn't need a gig ever again. And he wasn't sure he wanted to get involved with Nick Brand again. There were too many feelings to sort out.

Maybe it was time to take that long, long, extended vacation. Head down to the Keys, hook up with a couple of friends, fish, lay around, find some beach bunny, drink Kalick beer, and forget about rock and roll for a while. Maybe now was a good time to . . .

"Mick? You there? Whadda ya say? Huh?"

"Can't do it, Jamie. I'm sorry, man, but it just isn't that tempting."

"Shit. Name your price, Mick. What's it gonna take?"

"Jamie, as callous as this sounds, I don't need the money. What I need is a long break. That's what I need." He placed the phone in the receiver and pushed himself from the table. He needed to look up the phone number of a friend down in No Name Key. Buzz had a little bar and motel business called

Backwater. He'd make a reservation right now, fly down tomorrow morning, and hell, if it felt good he might not come back for a month or two. It would be the perfect place to get away from everything.

Chapter Two

October 29th, 4:30 A.M.

The buzzing reminded him of a swarm of bees. The alarm next to his bed was louder than he'd ever remembered it. Music wouldn't wake him up, so he'd purchased the loudest damned alarm clock he could find, and it worked. He reached over and banged the clock with his fist, silencing the menacing machine.

He crawled out of bed, actually happy that he'd turned down a nightcap and who knows what else with the young lady next door. He'd never have made the early-morning flight. She'd get over it.

Sever stripped off the boxer shorts and stood naked under the hot pounding shower, letting it beat life into his listless body. The blood began to circulate and he started to feel good about the day. Stepping out, he toweled and pulled on a pair of faded Levi's, a blue oxford cloth shirt, and slipped on a pair of brown Top-Siders. He checked the porch for a copy of the

Trib, but it was still too early. He glanced at his Rolex. The limo would take just about an hour to get to the airport. He'd have plenty of time to grab a paper and catch the 7:15 flight to Miami. He'd rent a car, maybe a convertible, and drive on down where the ocean breeze would blow through his hair and blow away every care he had. He needed to air everything out. Oh, this was going to be one hell of a relaxing vacation. Something he'd had coming for a long, long time.

Traffic was lighter than normal and they made O'Hare in fifty minutes. Sever tipped the driver well, dropped his bags off with the staff at the curb, and walked to the gate.

The young flight attendant flashed him a bright, toothy smile as she printed out his boarding pass. "I'm working first class today. If there's anything I can do for you, let me know."

Sever wasn't sure if she recognized him, or if it was just her good-natured attitude. It was almost too early in the morning for a come-on. Almost. He set off in search of the nearest newspaper. Four gates down he found one. The *Chicago Tribune* early edition front-page headline announced "Alderman Perry Indicted on Bribery Charges." Shit. He assumed that half the politicians in Chicago were on the take, so who cared if one of them wanted to give a little back to somebody? Maybe the late edition would have a headline that really grabbed his attention. With the world situation the way it was, anything was possible. He folded the paper under his arm, grabbed a *USA Today*, paid the lady with the sleepy eyes, and headed for the gate. Florida was starting to sound better and better.

Chapter Three

The flight to Atlanta was smooth, and he dozed over Ohio and Kentucky. He sipped a china cup of hot black coffee over Tennessee and was wide awake when they landed in Georgia. A one-hour layover was doable and he spent forty-five minutes in the Atlanta airport bookstore/deli that featured a variety of hardbacks and paperbacks. His newest release was prominently displayed on a round wooden table in the center of the room.

Sever couldn't help but smile. Jimmy Buffet had written a song that was very apropos for this occasion. The title was "I Heard I Was in Town." He seemed to precede himself in every town he visited. As many times as it happened, it still amused him. He picked up a copy of the book and studied the picture on the inside of the dust jacket. There stood a brooding, handsome man wearing comfortable clothes that hung loosely on what appeared to be a good physique for a man of his age. His full head of blond hair was moderately long, swept carelessly over his forehead, pushed back over his ears. Traces of gray appeared at his temples, and he seemed to be watching a disturbing scene somewhere off-camera. He couldn't remember what, or when the picture had been taken. It seemed years ago.

A television screen above the counter announced the overnight news as he browsed the periodicals. Something about a political scandal in Chicago. He knew all about it. He was headed toward the gate when the CNN anchor announced the breaking headline.

"In a late-breaking story, CNN has just learned that Florida congressman Robert Shapply was found this morning brutally murdered last night outside his Washington townhouse."

Sever spun around and stared at the screen.

"Officials confirm the body found on the steps is that of the congressman, who has been featured in the news and on this channel in recent weeks due to upcoming hearings on pornography in the music industry. Congressman Shapply's death was apparently caused by a gunshot wound to the head. An anonymous source said that identification had to be done using fingerprints. The face, according to the source, was unrecognizable."

Sever slowly walked to a chair, his knee throbbing and a slight limp in his gait. He slumped down on the seat and stared at the television. His eyes watched the anchor. His ears heard the voice. His thoughts drifted back to the last time he'd seen the congressman, and the last time he'd seen and talked to Nick Brand. The father and stepson had almost bankrupted him even while Nick had professed to be his best friend. He closed his eyes and massaged his temples with his hands, the conflicting emotions overwhelming him. They'd driven off in a stretch limousine as he stood on the curb and watched them disappear. They were much richer, and Sever was much poorer.

"While Charles White, the congressman's chauffeur, has been called in for questioning, police say he is not a suspect at this time. White was the last person known to see Shapply alive. Stay tuned to CNN for all the latest developments."

Sever stood up and stared into the distance, not seeing a thing. He was shell-shocked. He'd had vague thoughts about killing the man himself, and maybe killing the man's stepson. The two of them had worked him over better than anyone. His financial affairs had been devastated and as far as Sever was concerned, Brand was lucky he wasn't behind bars. Sever had trusted his lifelong friend, and Brand had stolen in excess of a million dollars. When Sever's $200-an-hour accountant had finished his report, some $12,000 later, he'd given Sever an estimate of about one and a half million dollars that Brand and his stepfather had been able to squirrel away. Sever was livid, but his $300-an-hour attorney, another $20,000 later, convinced him that there was little he could do.

Shapply and son had parted company, the soon-to-be congressman telling friends that he'd seen what the entertainment industry could do to people, how it could turn them into greedy bastards. He'd experienced a transformation of biblical proportions, and with the help of his wife's brother, the Reverend Joseph Evans, he'd run for Congress, threatening to expose the evils of Hollywood and rock and roll. And he'd won. You *can* fool all of the people some of the time.

Sever thought about calling Ginny. When someone is stealing two of you blind, you tend to bond over the misfortune and those financial problems had kept a very bad marriage together for two years longer than it should have. When the accountant and the attorney agreed that Sever and Ginny had no inexpensive recourse, they had set aside the legal threats, and set aside the marriage. The financial ramifications would be an issue for years to come.

A million thoughts flooded his mind. Sever pulled out a small notepad from his pants pocket and a pen from his shirt pocket. He titled the top of the page simply "Shapply." He numbered the sides of the paper and filled in the lines.

1) Call Nick Brand?
2) Funeral?
3) Call Ginny?
4) Call Jamie Jordan? Story?
5) Washington?
6) Go to Key West and forget the whole thing?

He massaged his throbbing knee, the pain shooting into the muscle of his thigh. Sometimes the aching distracted him. Now it helped him focus. Glancing at the clock, he realized he had a plane to catch, and glancing at the notes, he decided the Keys could wait. After all, waiting for something good, building up that anticipation for something that was out of reach just made it that much more tantalizing.

Gradually Sever became aware of the bustle around him. A lady with a large suitcase on wheels brushed by him, nearly knocking a magazine rack to the floor. The long line at the deli counter seemed longer by the minute, busy executives impatiently looking at their watches, reading front-page articles in the *Wall Street Journal*, and putting extra mustard on their corned beef and rye. Tired old ladies, sitting at small round tables, waited for their tired old friend or husband to bring them a salad and a Coke. A young couple by the entrance argued over who would watch the luggage and who would order the food.

Nobody cared about the congressman. And Sever wondered why *he* should, but deep down inside he knew. Somewhere in that murder there was a story. And he had the background to possibly do it justice. So it was Have-Laptop-Will-Travel. And in the course of this story, he knew he would run into Nick. Damn. That was going to be a tough meeting.

He picked up his leather carry-on and slowly walked to the bank of pay phones on the wall. Someday he was going to take a long, extended vacation. Maybe even go down to the Keys and just hang out. Someday. Right now there was a story to write.

Chapter Four

Jordan met him at the Baltimore airport. "Hell, this isn't that far, Mick. Since they limited flights into Reagan, everybody's getting used to it. This is like a suburb of Washington." The short, perky journalist nodded his head. "Yep, I'm sure glad you're on board. You've got to understand that this is a feather in my cap. I owe you, man! I owe you."

"Turn of events, Jamie. I was on my way to the Keys."

"Well, if it sells newspapers, then I'm in favor of it." Jamie chewed hard on what appeared to be a piece of stale peppermint gum. "I'm just glad we're friends, Mick."

Sever looked over at him, with the jelled hair that looked like he'd just gotten out of bed, and the sparse three-day growth on his cherubic face. The young man sported a leather blazer and a tan that meant he spent too much time in the Caribbean or too much time in a tanning booth. Twenty-five at the most. Sever himself had been as naïve, and as optimistic at twenty-five. At least he thought he was. Hell, it was too long ago to remember. At twenty-five he'd been syndicated in hundreds of newspapers nationwide and was one of the primary forces in defining the modern music industry. This guy was on the right career path—editor of the entertainment section of a major New York publication, and just as hungry as Sever imagined he'd been back then. The only thing the kid had wrong was the "friend" reference. Sever tried very hard not to have a friend in the business. It always caused problems. And then, as he thought about it, he realized that he didn't have too many friends in any other businesses either. Oh, people liked him. Sometimes too much, but he stayed aloof. A journalist had to remain objective. Friends could compromise your story. That was the excuse. Not a very good one, but one that worked when he was called upon to produce one.

"And it took us all by total surprise. I mean, hell, we were looking forward to a couple months of 'the music industry vs. the Shapplys.'" Jordan had been carrying on, his eyes darting from Sever to the road and back again. "I mean, when I told the publisher that you had called, they about shit their drawers, Mick. So what background stuff do you want from us?"

"I don't know yet. I knew the congressman. And I knew his son. I knew Alicia Shapply, but I never met the Reverend Joseph."

"Colorful guy. Shapply gives him the credit for turning his life around. But since Shapply got elected to Congress, nobody's heard much about him. Now, Evans seems to have talked him into this campaign against the entertainment industry. Maybe he thought it would put him back on top."

"And he got Shapply to go along with it."

"He did."

"Hell, the congressman was as bad as some of the people

he used to represent." Sever stared ahead. "So Shapply is doing a complete turnaround. Biting the hand that used to feed him."

"So to speak. I used to think he used Evans to get into political life, then ditched him. But now, I don't know. They were back together on this project, and Shapply was giving all the credit to the Reverend." Jordan slipped on a pair of sunglasses as the sun's brilliant orange fireball escaped from a bank of clouds and bounced blinding rays off the windshield. "You were in business with Shapply and his stepson, right?"

Sever was silent. He didn't care to reminisce.

"I don't mean to bring up bad news, but that's what I heard. Mind if I smoke?"

Without waiting for an answer, Jordan rolled down the window, spit out the gum, and pulled a low-tar filtered cigarette from his shirt pocket. He struck his lighter and inhaled the dirty, yellow-white smoke. Sever breathed a little deeper. He hadn't smoked a cigarette in two years, but the temptation was always there. Cigars once in a while, but no cigarettes.

"Jamie, if I decide to cover this story for your newspaper, I'll pick my own angle. I'll pick my own time, and I'll write it the way I see it. If at any time you don't agree with my style, I'm out of here. Okay?"

"Whatever you decide, Mick. They've given me permission to offer you whatever you want." He hesitated. "Within reason. We want your insight. We want your analysis."

"You want my byline."

"Yeah." Jamie grinned sheepishly as he blew a stream of smoke out the window. "We do want that."

"I'm not cheap."

"We know that."

"I take my time, but I am a professional and I'll work with you on a deadline."

"Glad to hear it."

"I want free rein to call on whoever I need to. I want someone to work with me on this story, someone of my choosing."

"We've got some great people on staff who would volunteer. Hell, Mick, the whole staff would give their eyeteeth to volunteer on a project like this with you. You've got a hell of a reputation."

"I'm thinking of someone outside your paper."

"Whatever you need."

Sever eased back into the soft leather seat of the Lexus. He wondered if she'd agree to work with him again. Ginny would be the first call he'd make when they got to the hotel.

Chapter Five

Washington hadn't changed that much. He'd half expected to see armed guards on every street corner, but that wasn't the case. There seemed to be quite a few police cars on the streets, but maybe he was just more aware of their presence.

"Can we drive by the Pentagon?"

"It's a little out of the way, but sure." Twenty minutes later Jordan drove by the building, pointing out the gaping hole. "Life goes on, Mick."

"And so does death. It's what happens in between life and death that I worry about."

Concrete barriers surrounded white government buildings and monuments. Cold, hard, and gray, they served as silent sentries guarding against unknown enemies. The occasional security van and police car were parked nearby, and side streets had been permanently blocked off, but the city still kept its European charm with its wide avenues and historic architecture. Parisian architect Pierre L'Enfant's vision still remained. The blue water of the Potomac caught the fiery red of the afternoon sun and for a moment looked like a molten river of hot lava twisting along its path. Brightly colored leaves were turning yellow, red, orange, and brown and the city appeared more beautiful than he'd remembered.

"You're from here, right?" They were passing Union Station.

"Yeah. Born here, but of course the job's in New York." Jordan tossed his second cigarette out the window and pointed to the left. "Your hotel is right up there. You're within walking distance of the Capitol."

"You'll be around for a couple of days?"

"Sure. If you need anything . . ."

"I'll probably need to get my bearings. It's been a while since I was here last."

"No problem. Whatever you need. I'm staying in Georgetown with some friends, so whatever you want, just let me know."

"Your city looks great."

"Yeah, I think so. Not to sound sappy, but fall is my favorite time of the year here. Tourists always want the cherry blossoms. Me, I like it when the leaves change color. Puts some serious personality into the city." Jordan checked his watch and flipped on the radio. "Top of the hour. See if they're still opening with it."

A commercial was winding up. The sounder for headline news opened and faded as the announcer introduced herself. "In a dramatic turn of events, two suspects have been arrested in the brutal murder of Congressman Robert Shapply. The first arrest came about one hour ago in New York City. John

Wesley Whittier, the rapper known as Chilli D, was arrested in his apartment on Fifth Avenue. Whittier was known to be one of the artists targeted by the late Robert Shapply. The second arrest was made just minutes ago. We switch you live to Brad Thomas outside the second-district headquarters on Idaho Avenue."

"Judy, ten minutes ago police brought in the second suspect in the murder of Congressman Shapply. I think it's safe to say that everyone here is stunned. The suspect is Nicky Brand, Shapply's stepson and former business partner."

Sever stared at the radio as if he could will it to spill the rest of the story.

"No motive has been given in either arrest, but Brand's mother, Alicia Shapply, walked in just moments ago and we expect some sort of press conference in the immediate future. I'll have more as soon as we hear anything."

"Thank you, Brad. In other news—" Jordan turned off the radio.

"Jeez! It gets stranger and stranger, doesn't it. Here's your hotel, Mick."

"Get me down to the second district."

"You don't want to—"

Sever pointed ahead. "Go!"

"You got it." He pulled back into traffic and he stepped on the gas, squealing the tires for emphasis.

Chapter Six

Nobody came between them. Biological twins were never as close as Mick and Nick. Friends called them the M and N twins, and people who didn't like them called them weird. They'd met at age thirteen, too late in life for childhood memories but at an age when teenage angst was rearing its ugly head. The two boys helped each other through the tough times and celebrated the good. And there were some good times!

Sever came from middle-class parents, living with a father who occasionally beat up Sever's mother. Brand was the product of a broken marriage and a father he never knew. He grew up in the lap of luxury, with a wealthy industrialist stepfather who occasionally beat up his wife and his stepson. Sever had the talent, Brand had the money, and both boys had the looks. At age fifteen you could look at the two boys and see there was something very special about their relationship. Either they were going to be major trouble, or their charm would change the world. Both views seemed to be correct.

Brand had the cash to buy drugs and alcohol, and the two teens spent a great deal of time experimenting with both. Mick and Nick found that good looks, personality, and drugs and alcohol endeared them to their peer group, especially the young, attractive, long-legged girls. There was a hell of a lot of experimenting with them, too.

They shared girlfriends, sometimes simultaneously—same girl, same bed, same time. Sometimes behind the other one's back, and more often than not the act was just to share the experience, because the M and N twins shared everything. Except Ginny.

Sever felt certain that Nick Brand had never been intimate with Ginny. When Nick realized the special bond that Sever and Ginny seemed to share, he backed off. He was never happy about Sever suddenly splitting his allegiances, but he seemed to understand there was something different about this relationship. And at least at that stage in their life and relationship, Ginny would never have screwed around on him. Not at that stage. Sever, on the other hand, never let a serious relationship get in the way of having a good time. A jumble of thoughts crowded his head as Jordan pulled up to the jail.

"We'll hold him here until we can arraign him in court, sometime in the next twenty-four hours. And no, you can't see him. His attorney is the only person we'll allow in there right now." The bald sergeant with the garish yellow tie glanced down at the sheet of paper in front of him, working on it with his pen, dismissing Sever by ignoring him.

"Will he make bail?"

The officer raised his eyes and squinted at Sever. "We don't arrest 'em unless we think we can hold 'em. And if we've got enough to arrest them, they're likely to be a flight risk. So chances are pretty slim that he'll make bail."

"Maybe a high bail? This guy has more money than God."

"Well, sir, if they've got money then they're *really* a flight risk."

Sever glanced over at Jordan. He was paying rapt attention, watching the expert at work. Sever could almost sense his anticipation, waiting for the award-winning journalist to charm the old desk cop and arrange the in-jail interview. He was sorry to disappoint the young man, but this one wasn't going to happen just yet.

"Thank you for your time. I assume he'll be at the central facility after the hearing?" The sergeant nodded without looking up. That was the end of that.

They walked slowly back to the Lexus. Jordan sucked on his cigarette, blowing short puffs of smoke from the side of his mouth. "Do you get pumped up when you start working on a story like this?"

"Pumped up?"

"Yeah. I mean, this isn't like some personality feature about some new rock star, or some review of a new CD. This is edgy stuff. I feel this energy. I'm pumped."

"I want to find out what happened. That's all."

"No excitement? No energy?"

"No." He lied. His blood was flowing faster already.

"Did you ever feel that way?"

"I don't know. I just know that I want to find out what happened. And I will."

"Who killed him and why. Just get down to business, right?"

"That, too."

"What else is there?"

"I want to find out what happened to a friendship. I may have waited too long."

Chapter Seven

Word spread fast. The answering machine was loaded with calls from everyone, including Ginny.

"Hey, babe, have you heard about Nicky? He's a suspect in his daddy's murder. Call me."

His current business agent had called. Then there were two associates at the *Florida Sun Coast* who were fishing for some leads, a reporter he knew at the *Chicago Tribune*, a handful of rock acts that had suffered the same financial fate that he had, and his editor. They all left messages, wanting to be the first to tell him. The call that interested him the most was from Chilli D's producer and manager. He decided to return that call.

"T-Beau? Is that you?"

"It's me. 'Sup, Top Dawg?"

"I bet you say that to all the guys."

"Naw. You were there for me, Mick. When we was startin' out, you know what I'm sayin'? You were *top* dawg. Still are."

His deep rich baritone voice rolled out of the receiver and Sever could picture the big man on the other end. On stage with his colorful do-wrag wrapped carefully around his head, his barrel chest, and the gold warm-up suit. And Sever was sure that T-Beau even slept in his gold chains. The man must have had twenty of them around his thick black neck. And twenty gold records. Probably watched a lot of *The A-Team* on television back in the eighties. T-Beau was bigger than life. He'd ride onto stage on a sparkling Gold Harley Davidson, and the magic would begin.

"T-Beau, you called me."

"I did. Seems I got a big problem here. My boy Chilli, they're accusing him of murder."

"Did he do it?"

"The reason I'm callin' you? Nicky Brand was your friend. Am I right? Now, what do you know?"

"You're in New York?"

"I am."

"I'm in Washington right now. I'm thinking about doing a story on the murder, a little background on Brand and his dad, try to get a handle on what Shapply and his wife were going to do at these hearings."

"Hey, Mick, you think Chill will be extradited? How soon?"

"I don't know, but I'd guess they'll want him here in the next forty-eight. They'll file the paperwork, and if his attorney doesn't fight it he could be here by tomorrow."

"I don't trust Chill's attorney. White guy named Freddy. I need to know if my man was guilty. Got a friend with a Lear Jet. I'll be in D.C. tomorrow morning. Any chance we can hook up?"

"Sure. I'm at the Essex. Call me when you get in."

"You'll be number one. You know what I'm sayin'?"

Sever hung up the phone, already missing the deep rumbling voice. It used to be you couldn't turn on the radio without hearing it. T-Beau had moved on. Instead of being the talent, he produced new talent. And put out fires. This one appeared to be very hot.

Chapter Eight

Washington, D.C. why am I not surprised?" The soft voice of his ex-wife almost whispered over the several thousand miles. "You heard about it and couldn't stay away."

"I noticed you were on top of it, too."

"Hey, babe, that man took a lot of money from us. I hate to see something like this happen, but maybe somebody decided to take matters into his own hands."

"Do you know Chilli D?" Sever took a mouthful of his smooth Scotch, let it caress his tongue, and leaned back into the foam-rubber pillow on his king-size bed. The vast space seemed wasted. He pictured Ginny next to him. Nice picture.

"I ran him up on the computer. Did time for a murder in Texas, and there were stories about some major police brutality. When he got out of jail he had a couple of minor hits with Puffy. He left Combs and produced one on his own. Not very successful. The record company dumped him. T-Beau is working with him now, trying to jump-start his career, telling everyone that Chilli will be the next Snoop. Seems he's got some new stuff with a hard edge. It's hard to tell the players anymore, Mick. However, I did get a lead on the connection."

"Let me guess. Nicky was his business adviser." He could picture her, sitting in her apartment, probably a T-shirt, blue jeans, and bare feet, her blond hair smelling like jasmine.

"That's it. You and I are on the same . . ."

"We've always been on the same."

"Wavelength. I know. If that was all there was to it . . ."

"Ginny, I'm going to do the story. Do you want to fly in and work with me?"

There was silence on the other end. He could see her chewing on the end of a pencil.

"You want to think about it? You know these things break fast. I need someone to do a little research, someone who is—"

"On the same wavelength. Shit, Sever. There's never a good time. I've got a deadline on a new writer and I've got to edit his piece for a release in the next two weeks."

"So? You're a great editor. You can do it here, and work on this story when you get time."

"You're always so understanding. Never any pressure!" Her sarcasm was biting.

"Look, I work better when you're here. There might be another book in this. You've never complained about the money."

"It's not about the money. It's about the obligation. Let me make a couple of calls. Obviously this is one story I've got a personal interest in—I mean, Nick and everything. Let me call you back. One hour."

He hung up the phone and flipped on the TV, rolling the

taste of Scotch over his tongue. Thank God for hotel mini-bars. And thank God for live news. Instant news was great! You didn't have to go to the press conference. You could sip Scotch, talk to the love of your life, and still get all the details as they happened.

"Mrs. Shapply, have you talked to your son?" The Fox News camera was trained on Alicia Shapply.

She stood stoic, reserved, the Ice Maiden. That's what they'd called her, the M and N twins, behind her back. The Ice Maiden. She never cracked.

"No. I'm certain you know where Nick is at this moment, and until he is arraigned I will have no communication with him."

"Mrs. Shapply. Were you in Sarasota when you heard about this?"

"Yes." She wore a gray suit, and a high-collared blue blouse under the tailored gray jacket. The camera zoomed in and he could see the strain on her seventy-four-year-old face. It appeared the Ice Maiden might melt.

"With all respect to your deceased husband," the reporter said, pausing, "do you feel that the upcoming hearings were in some way responsible for his"—again there was an uncomfortable pause—"untimely death?"

"For his murder?"

"Uh, yeah."

She gripped the podium as if for support. "My husband is dead. I don't know who is responsible. I . . . I am going through a lot of emotions right now." She turned from the camera, and Sever could swear the Ice Maiden was ready to thaw.

He poured the rest of the bottle into his glass, walked to

the sink, and added a splash of water. He could feel the alcohol in his veins, warming him up. He smiled at Alicia Shapply, thinking to himself that she really didn't have these emotions inside of her. When she turned back to the camera, tears were streaming down her face. He felt chagrined. This was about a woman's husband who'd been brutally murdered. Even an Ice Maiden would be emotional about that. And then it hit him. Alicia was to have been a partner in the hearings. She, her husband, and her brother, the Reverend Joseph Evans, had been set to bring the wrath of God down on the recording and video industry. Not only had she lost her husband, not only had her only son been accused of the murder, but what if she was a target, too?

"Ladies and gentlemen, that's all." A young man moved in, taking control of the microphones. Alicia was led off-camera and the focus returned to New York. "There you've seen the press conference for Alicia Shapply, live from Washington, D.C. In the short question-and-answer period—" Sever shut off the TV. He could provide his own commentary. He'd seen the conference. Now, he was worried about the well-being of the Ice Maiden.

Chapter Nine

She called him back in ten minutes. "I'm flying in tomorrow afternoon. You'd better have first-class accommodations, buddy boy. When you hire high-priced talent, be prepared to pay for it!" Sever smiled. He missed her. The players would be in tomorrow. T-Beau and Ginny. Jamie was already in place. Sometimes he felt like Peter Graves in the old *Mission Impossible* TV series. Not the Tom Cruise version, but the one with Graves, where he carefully analyzed the mission, then hired the team. It was always the same team, but they always got the job done.

He lay back on the bed, lacing his fingers behind his head. He stared at the ceiling and reviewed what he knew so far. Almost nothing. He was anxious to talk to Alicia Shapply, less anxious to talk to her son. Due to the nature of the charge, he was certain that Chilli D would be in Washington in a couple of days. Then the pieces would start to fall into place. Swinging his legs over the side of the bed, he sat up and got to his feet. The twinge in his knee made him sit back down for a second, and he massaged it. He needed a meal and a walk. His stomach needed food and his leg needed the exercise, and an evening walk around the nation's capital was something he hadn't done since he and Ginny had been here, about ten years ago. Maybe the two of them could do it again tomorrow.

Chapter Ten

The commotion in the hall woke him. The maids were making their appointed rounds at the ungodly hour of 8 A.M. He'd helped to close a couple of the capital city bars and really could use the sleep. Hotels were like hospitals. They told you to rest comfortably, then woke you up as early as possible to ask you if you had a good night's sleep. Now there were raised voices in Spanish and some dialect he couldn't make out. He pulled on a pair of jeans and went to the door. Peering through the hole, he could make out the maid, guarding her cart as someone off center apparently threatened her.

Sever opened the door and stepped into the hall. The five-foot maid was shaking her finger and screaming in Spanish at the six-foot-six black giant in front of her. The man held up a hand to silence her, a massive hand that looked like it could crush the tiny woman.

"Now, sister, you see if I've been lyin'. This here's my man, Mick." The big man took two steps toward Sever and threw his arms around him. “Hell, all I wanted to do was borrow the key, sneak in, and surprise your ass. Now sister Consuela, or whatever the fuck her name is, done spoiled it. You got a honey in there? I can leave.”

“No honey.” Sever maneuvered himself out of the tight bear hug, reached in his jeans pocket, found several bills folded together, pulled off a ten, and handed it to the small, middle-aged lady in the yellow uniform. “*Pardon. Gracias.*”

That pretty much covered his knowledge of the Spanish language. She did seem to understand the American currency and smiled at him, flashing an evil look at the big black man.

“*Gracias.*”

T-Beau shot a look back at her. “Bitch,” he muttered under his breath. The two men walked into the room. Sever glanced at him and noticed subtle differences from the T-Beau of old. The big guy didn’t wear a scarf in everyday life, and his shaved head sported a day’s growth, showing part of his hair turning silver. The six-foot-six frame that used to have the girls squealing in their seats had gotten softer and more rotund with age, and it would soon be hard for the big-and-tall shop to find his size. But the fortune this man had amassed over the years could probably afford him a custom tailor for the rest of his life. He wore a knit shirt, a silk sport coat with a pair of casual slacks, and spit-shined shoes. Not a gold chain to be seen.

“It’s been a while. Still charming the ladies, I see.” Sever pulled up a desk chair and sat down.

“You can’t please ’em all, Mick. How you been? I been readin’ your book on the Jamaican band. You doin’ alright for yourself.” The big man settled down on the edge of the bed, crushing the mattress under his large frame.

"And you?"

"Aw, you know. Workin' with uppity niggers who think they know everything about the business. Shit, they want it all handed to 'em on a platter, Mick. Don't want to work for nothin'. I get 'em a record deal and it goes to their head. Right now. Was I ever that bad?"

"You? Think you know everything? You always knew everything. But you worked for what you got. I remember. You worked hard!"

"Still do. And Chill, he's a hard worker, too, Mick. Lives large, but he's been around and he knows what it's gonna take. I think the boy has a future and I don't want to see him take a rap for somethin' he din't do."

"Let me get a quick shower and we'll go downstairs and grab some coffee." Sever walked to the bathroom.

"Mick, you know that Nicky Brand was managing Chill's money?" T-Beau shouted through the door.

"Yeah, I heard. After everything that happened, people still trust Nick Brand. Charm goes a long way."

"Well, Nicky was floatin' him some green. My boy needed cash. I knew what was happenin', but I didn't know how much."

Sever turned on the shower. He stripped off the jeans and underwear and stepped into the tub, feeling the hot, pulsating water beat a wakeup call on his skin. Three minutes later he stepped out, towled off, and pulled on the jeans and a blue oxford shirt. He stepped back into the main room. The black singer sat on the edge of the bed, watching a cartoon on the TV.

"Did you catch what I said about Chill?"

"Yeah. You said that Nicky was lending him some money."

"Lots of jack."

"How much?"

"Serious money. Two hundred fifty thou."

"Jeez. That's pretty serious. What was he going to do with that kind of money?"

"He's got his expenses. Chill lives pretty high, and anyway, we were gettin' ready to sign the boy up. Chilli's contract would have been worth four times that."

"Still," Sever ran the towel through his hair, slipped on a pair of Top-Siders, and motioned to the door.

They exited and headed for the elevators.

"You ain't seen the paper this morning?"

"No. I was peacefully sleeping when you started that commotion in the hall."

"The paper claims Chill was hired by Nicky Brand to kill the old man. They're sayin' Nicky Brand told Chill that if he murdered the congressman, that would be payment for the $250,000 loan."

"Hell of an expensive murder. Would Chilli have done it? Killed Shapply if he thought the debt was wiped clean?"

T-Beau was quiet for a moment. "You did your homework, you know this isn't his first brush with the law. Chill killed a man in Texas. Probably self-defense, but then he got beat up by some cops and it fucked him up pretty bad. Did time. So, do I think the boy could do it again? It's possible, you know what I'm sayin'? It's possible. Yeah."

Chapter Eleven

The waitress brought him six eggs and what appeared to be a pound of bacon. Sever could detect murmurs from around the room as the occasional patron recognized the big man.

"You still attract attention."

"You know, you can't be my size and not get noticed. But the oldie stations still play the songs, and once in a while they roll my ass out on some television special and I do my part." He chuckled a low, rumbling laugh.

"The Love Doctor. The music's changed since then."

"Still get that. All the time. 'Hey, doctor love! Can you make me better?' You gave me that name."

"You and Barry White. He did pretty well with that image, too."

"Shit, he's still doin' good. But me, I'm not complainin', you know what I'm sayin'? I had a good run. And, pardon the dig, but I put my money in some *safe* investments. Din't get into anything with the Nicky Brands of this world."

"So Nicky is now in the lending business?"

"Yeah. Two hundred fifty thou. Now my guess is that he knew Chill was signing, so he figured it was safe. Still, that puts my man in a beholdin' situation. You owe a man a couple hundred thou, you might do a favor to erase some of that debt."

"Why? Why did he need that much money?"

"He lives large, Mick. Got a big house, stable full of cars, got his women, there are several, and"—he hesitated—"and he always had a couple of bodyguards. After what he'd been through, he figured he needed some protection." He finished the last bite of egg, and mopped up the yolk with a piece of whole wheat toast.

"So why does Nicky Brand want to kill his stepfather?"

"To protect his business. Niggers talkin' 'bout the ghetto life, but they take in tons of cash, and live in the hills with their millions. Nicky Brand guides 'em through the world of investments."

"Obviously Nicky must be more successful than when I was with him." Sever gazed at his plate for a moment. "So with the old man threatening Nicky's customer base, it was time to whack the congressman and stop the hearings?"

"The congressman gets rich off the business, then gets religion. Somethin' about that never set right with me."

The lady approached the table, looking a little flustered as she palmed her paper napkin. "Excuse me, are you, well of course you are. Nobody else looks like . . ." She was mid-thirties, and about thirty pounds overweight, her overdyed red hair hanging in ringlets around her oval face. "Could you . . . would you sign an autograph?" She handed the napkin to

T-Beau. The big guy beamed, giving her a toothy smile.

"Of course, ma'am." He seemed to drop his voice an octave when he addressed her. "And how do you want me to sign it?"

"Uh, could you write 'To Rosie, from the Love Doctor?' Then just sign your name." She watched as he scribbled the message. "Oh, Hank is going to be sooo jealous!" She gave him a girlish laugh, took the napkin from his hand, and just for a moment looked into his eyes, as if she were hypnotized. She walked away, almost skipping.

"Lady gonna make love to Hank tonight thinkin' bout the Love Doctor. Hell, if I wasn't famous, that lady would be stayin' ten blocks away from me at all times. I'd be that woman's worst nightmare. Funny 'bout fame, you know what I'm sayin'? I'm gonna be in her dreams tonight."

Sever smiled. "So a lot of people are upset that Shapply turned on them. There's a good reason for murder. You're linked to some of those careers, too. Ever think about taking the congressman out?"

T-Beau hesitated and seemed to measure his response. "Naw. But there's a bunch of record companies, producers, and managers who wanted the congressman out of the way. There's a whole culture built up around this nasty business. A couple of years ago Eminem was in trouble for talkin' 'bout killin' his old lady. It's got ten times worse than that. Rape, kiddy rape, animals, they sing about some pretty nasty shit. Wife killin' and cop killin' don't even make the top ten! Lots of rappers makin' lots of money were hopin' Shapply would just drop out of sight. If Nicky and Chill didn't kill him, there are plenty of other suspects to choose from."

Sever nodded. "Maybe you."

"You had some reasons, too, Mick. A little revenge?"

"You're right. There were a lot of people who had it in for the congressman. What do you know about Reverend Joseph Evans?"

"Stories you read. Saved the congressman, taught him a new way of life. Hell, if you believe his press, this Evans character saved half the cons who walked out of prison. I never met the man. A lot of people swear by him, but you know me. I'm skeptical as hell." He glanced at his watch. "I got things to do, I'll catch up with you later, and if you hear anything about Chill, when he's gonna make his D.C. appearance, you let me know. I'm stayin' here, room 220." T-Beau stood up and seemed to keep standing up until his towering frame rose above the table like a statue. He reached into his pocket and pulled out a fifty and a ten.

"Fifty's for the meal. Ten is for the maid upstairs. I don't need anybody pickin' up my tab, 'specially you. You're my top dawg, Mick. You were there, and I'll never forget it. Man can't have too many friends." He walked away, and all eyes followed him.

Chapter Twelve

Jamie had called the room. "We need to get you a cell phone, Mick. Gotta be in touch. Call me."

No cell phone. He worked best when he wasn't in touch. When he wasn't under somebody's thumb. He hated cell phones. Sever had been dragged screaming and kicking into the computer age, for years preferring an electric portable typewriter. He'd finally found a laptop that he loved, but Palm Pilots and cell phones were not part of his package.

The second message surprised him. Totally. He wasn't aware that anyone even knew he was in town.

"Mick, this is Alicia Shapply. I understand you may be doing a story on the . . ." She paused, the word, the phrase, the idea seemed difficult to verbalize. ". . . on the murder of my husband. Since you had a relationship with my husband and son, I'd like very much to discuss this story with you. Please, do me this small favor and call me." She left her number.

Sever called Jamie.

"Hey, Mick. Got a cell phone all checked out for you. No charge. That way I can check in, see what kind of progress you're making."

Sever ignored him. "Jamie, get me some CDs. I can play them on the laptop. A couple by, I don't know, Ja Rule, OutKast, Bustah Rhymes, Wu-Tang, Ludacris, or anybody else that's current. And get me anything you can find on Chilli. Oh, and get me a greatest-hits CD of T-Beau."

"You think maybe the lyrics to some old T-Beau songs might be part of the hearing?"

"No. But pad the expense account. I want that one for me. I miss his old stuff."

"Okay, and Mick, I'll drop the cell phone off at—"

"No cell phone, Jamie. If I've got to have you covering me every minute, I'm off the story."

"Well, shit. How about you check in with me maybe twice a day just so I—"

"Jamie. Pay attention. I don't really need the story. I'll follow it through, but you've got to stay off of my back. You'll get some good stuff, I promise you. But if you're going to make demands, find somebody else to do the piece."

"Hey. We want you. I've got to ask, don't I? Don't want you pulling off the story. I'm sure this will work just fine."

Sever had threatened a lot of editors in his day. A lot of editors bigger than Jamie Jordan. But deep in his heart he knew this was one story he couldn't pull off of. No matter how much he threatened. He couldn't wait to see what the Ice Maiden wanted to talk about. He said good-bye to Jamie and dialed Alicia Shapply's number.

Chapter Thirteen

The white limo was waiting outside, just like she'd promised. The uniformed chauffeur opened the door and Sever slid in. She sat across from him in a tan leather captain's chair, looking elegant and aloof, her stylish gray hair framing her carefully sculpted face. Sever knew that thousands of dollars had been spent to shape that face and tighten the skin on the Ice Maiden. She wore a black dress, modestly long, and the collar rose up, accenting her delicate neck. Her jewelry consisted of a simple strand of pearls, and he noticed the ever-present diamond tennis bracelet on her wrist. Nick had once told him that the carat weight was something like ten. Her wedding ring, a delicate band of white gold, sported a three-carat, pear-shaped diamond. Alicia Shapply was the definition of elegance and abundance.

"Mrs. Shapply. It's been a long time."

She gave him a polite smile, her perfectly capped teeth a lethal white against the even tan of her skin. "Mick. The last time I saw you, I believe you were with your lovely wife, Virginia? You were visiting Nick, in Sarasota."

"Yeah. Listen, I'm really sorry about your husband. And I don't know what to say about Nick. I—"

The limousine left the curb and Alicia Shapply held up her hand. "Charlie's going to drive around the city for a while. This way we can have a little more privacy. Would you like a drink?" She motioned to a side bar.

"No."

"Charlie was Robert's chauffeur." She poured herself a small amount of vodka, added three ice cubes, and took a sip. "You don't have to give me any sympathy. I know the problems that you and my son had. While I have my own idea of what may have happened, I felt very bad about the deterioration of your relationship with Nick. You two were very good friends. You see, Nick still considers you to be his best friend."

Sever was quiet, looking into her eyes, totally taken aback by the statement. They passed the Capitol, security cars parked at the entrances. Finally he spoke. "Mrs. Shapply, I'm not really sure what you wanted to discuss."

"Do you remember Amber? Nick's sister?"

"Sure. What was she, about four or five years younger than Nick? I think she was maybe eleven or twelve when we were sixteen."

"Exactly. Five years younger than Nick. She was his half sister. This is very difficult for me, and very complicated. You see, she and her father, the congressman, they're . . . they weren't very close. In fact, they hadn't talked in the last several years."

Sever was quiet, letting the lady tell the story at her own pace. He had the feeling that she needed to set him up, have him take sides on an issue that he really didn't have any interest in. He'd been in too many interview situations. He could feel it when the interviewee was leading him. The comment about him being Nick's best friend and now about the sister—the Ice Maiden was leading him. He just didn't know where.

"Amber is somewhat bitter. She's in her thirties, and things have not gone that well for her. I think she blames her father, possibly the lack of his interest in her. She's had one failed marriage and she has a daughter, Margarite. She named her after a childhood friend."

"Margarite. Margarite Haller. She was molested and murdered. I remember that story. Years ago." He noticed Alicia's eyes narrow. Her hand seemed to tremble, and she put the vodka to her lips and took a long sip.

"Yes. I thought you might remember. Anyway, Amber has named her daughter after her childhood friend. Totally against my wishes. And now, with her father murdered, I'm afraid the strain on her may be too much. Through friends, I've found that she is hiring a lawyer to review her father's will. She apparently does not feel that she or Margarite have been properly provided for."

"Mrs. Shapply, what does this have to do with your husband's murder, or Nick being in jail? I don't mean to be rude, but this sounds like family business to me. Something I shouldn't be involved with."

"I told you, this was difficult to tell. To be as brief as possible, while I grieve for my husband, I feel very strongly that our governor will, if I ask, appoint me to serve out my husband's term. I am very involved in Florida causes, and I feel very dedicated to Robert's crusade against the entertainment industry. I intend to continue his work." She swallowed the rest of her vodka and seemed to be more focused and firm. "Amber can stir up a lot of trouble. She always looked up to Nick, and I think he can settle her down."

"For God's sake, he's in jail for the murder of your husband."

She gave him her polite, standoffish smile. "Nick had nothing to do with Robert's death. I know that. You know that. I'm certain that he'll be out in a matter of days." She spoke with the air of someone who was used to privilege and rank, and with the confidence of someone who was used to getting her own way. "I know you'll be seeing Nick in the next day or two and I'd like you to ask him if he would talk to his sister. Ask her to leave things alone until we get this dreaded thing behind us. I think he'll listen to you, and I think she'll listen to him."

"Mrs. Shapply, when is the last time you spoke to your daughter, Amber?"

She hesitated. "It may have been a year or more."

"And Nick? When was the last time you spoke to him?"

"We talk. At holidays, possibly last Christmas. Do you think you can ask him? He needs to tell Amber to leave it alone. This is extremely important."

"Why don't you?"

"He'll listen to you."

"We don't talk. At all."

"I understand this comes as a shock to you, but I stand by my statement. I know that my son still considers you his best friend."

He watched her face for some sign of insincerity. "Mrs. Shapply—"

"He respects you immensely. When you talk to him, I feel certain you'll see what I mean. I need you to"—she looked coldly into his eyes—"intercede for me."

Still the Ice Maiden. Her ability to communicate with anyone with a warm, human emotion seemed remote. She had locked out her children. Her only concern was how they might affect her chances for future success. Sever stared out the window, watching the reds, greens, and golds along the Potomac. All his life he'd heard the term "inside the Beltway" to describe the isolation of political figures from the rest of the world. People who only worked for their own common good, insulated from the affairs and concerns of the general population. Here was a woman caught up in her own world, inside the Beltway. Inside Alicia Shapply.

"Are you planning on holding the hearings?"

"Oh, yes. We will have the hearings. My brother Joseph and I will see to that. Please, Mick. Ask Nick to have a talk with his sister. Tell her to leave it alone. It's important to me."

A motorcycle roared by, and Sever could see the leather-jacketed driver, the visor on his helmet down as he swerved in front of the limo, then pulled out and took a right off the main road.

He heard the bang and felt the car swerve. A tire blowing out at forty-five miles an hour in the middle of rush-hour traffic. Charlie seemed to be struggling, trying to straighten the car, pulling on the steering wheel, then the wheel ripped free from his hands and the car careened onto the median strip with a loud screeching sound, hanging up on the curb for a second, tires spinning and burning against the concrete, the vehicle leaping forward and smashing into a tree, the hood springing open, and steam rolling from the engine. It happened in a brief moment and the severe shock of the crash shook Sever for several seconds. He felt the pain in his knee and it helped clear his head. Sever grabbed Alicia Shapply and pulled her out of the seat, pushed her out the door, and urged her to keep going. She stumbled away and he hobbled back, desperately jerking on the jammed driver's door, trying to open it. Finally, he limped to the passenger door, pulled it open, and reached for the driver. Blood trickled from the hole below Charlie White's left eye. A hole that had nothing to do with a car crash. Sever recognized a bullet wound when he saw it. And as he tugged on the body, trying to pull it from the car, he noticed the windshield, a perfect hole in the center with the spider veins going in all directions. There was no flat tire. Either the chauffeur had some serious enemies or someone was trying to kill him or the Ice Maiden. He had a hunch they were after her.

Chapter Fourteen

So, Mick, you really know how to treat a girl. I come all the way from Chicago and have to meet you in a hospital."

Sever glanced up in surprise. A smile tugged at the corners of his mouth, a smile he couldn't stop. She always did that to him. It was probably the same smile that he'd tragically stolen from her several years ago. There was joy and sadness in that smile and she knew it. She could read him like a book. Here she was, Ginny, with the long blond hair, the blue eyes that held a mischievous twinkle. Ginny, who could still hit his hot buttons. Almost every one of them. The waiting room had just gotten very small.

"Hey. You're here."

"Ah, ever the wordsmith." She grinned and held out her arms.

He reached out and gave her a hug, going for a kiss, but she turned her cheek to him. "So, babe, what the hell is going on here? The hotel said you were at the hospital and I assumed—"

"That I was hurt, sick, whatever."

"Mick, you do get yourself into a lot of shit."

"Yeah. And I think I may have stepped into it again. I just finished debriefing the cops. Alicia Shapply is being treated for some minor cuts and bruises. We were in a limo together and—"

"You? And the Ice Maiden? Maybe you'd better start from the beginning. I've got to hear this one."

Sever put down the magazine and ran a hand through his hair. "They've got a coffee shop down the hall. Let's go."

"So if Chilli D is the hired killer, and he's in jail, then who took a shot at you and Mrs. Shapply? And if Nicky is in jail, then how could he hire another shooter?" Her half cup of coffee had gone cold as she'd listened and hung on every word. Ginny was good at listening. She was a good listener, a good research assistant, a good editor, and had been a pretty good wife. Probably a lot better than he ever deserved.

"Somebody wants the Shapplys out of the picture. That's the only answer. Somebody other than the people who are in jail. The possibilities are endless. If these hearings have any credibility a lot of people are going to be in the hot seat. I mean record companies, rap artists, managers . . ."

"Business managers. Like Nicky."

"Yeah. Like Nicky. Alicia looked at me and said, 'You know Nick didn't have anything to do with this.' What do you think?"

"Mick, that was then. The M and N twins are history.

People constantly evolve and you can't tell what they're going to do. The old Nicky Brand was a good guy. A true friend. But he changed. He showed his new stripes when he stole our money. Evolution isn't always a good thing."

"We could argue that point. I'm not sure people change."

"Some people don't. I'm not sure you have." She looked into his eyes and gave him a half smile. "You still have this amazing drive to get the story. You can't just sit back and savor the fruits of your labor."

"The fruits of my labor? We're not talking about an orchard here. We're talking about the murder of a friend's stepfather, and—"

"A *former* friend's stepfather. He changed. It wouldn't surprise me to find out he did hire someone to kill the congressman."

Sever played with the handle on his cup. He swirled the murky black liquid inside, then shoved it aside. "I've got to put together a list of the people they were going to have testify at these hearings. I've got to get an interview with Chilli, got to talk to the Ice Maiden again, have a meeting with T-Beau, and . . ."

"And have that dreaded meeting with Nicky Brand. I'd like to sit in on that one, but I think it would be better if I didn't. First of all, I think you two need to be alone for a while, and second, Nicky had a crush on me and I don't think—"

"He had a crush on everyone I ever dated. But in your case he never did anything about it." He looked at her with a questioning glance, waiting to see if she gave him validation. She was silent. "Anyway, there's a lot of work to be done. The police have no clue who took out the limo driver, and Mrs.

Shapply just got into town so she's clueless as well."

"So how did they get Chilli and Nick? Tell me again."

The waitress approached the table, asking about refills. They both declined and Sever folded his hands together. "One of the news channels claims the cops found Chilli D's itinerary. New York to Washington and back to New York—same day. Chilli D tells a friend that he is paying off a loan to his manager and the payoff could involve someone getting killed. Sounds to me like a brag from a rapper who wants to come off as street smart."

"So the friend, who may not be that good a friend, hears about the murder and calls the police?"

"That's it."

"I hope they have more to go on than that."

"They do. He kept the weapon. Not too bright. They found it in his apartment. It sounds to me like they've got him dead to rights. And you know he's been up for murder before."

"Then who tried to kill Mrs. Shapply?"

"Chilli may have set it up, or maybe we've got two killers. Apparently there are a lot of people who would like to see the Shapplys dead."

"Well, kiddo"—she laced her fingers in front of her and gave him a hard stare—"we've got our work cut out for us, and I've got one week to spend on it."

"We'd better get busy."

"My thoughts exactly."

"One more thing," Sever said. "She mentioned Amber. Remember Amber?"

"Sure. Amber, the sister. That was a big deal. She had the girlfriend, Margarite somebody, who was killed?"

"Yeah. Over in Barbados. Made big headlines, and I'm not sure what happened. It turns out Amber named her daughter Margarite. Anyway, Alicia says that Amber could make trouble for her. Something about contesting the will, I don't know. She seemed obsessed with me telling Nicky that he needed to talk to Amber and settle her down. Some sort of family matter."

"You're kidding. You get screwed out of one and a half million dollars, and the first thing she wants you to say to your former friend is, 'tell your sister to leave your mom alone'? This woman is certifiable."

"She wants a shot at taking her husband's spot. Thinks she can get the governor to give it to her. You've got to understand this lady. She's got all the class money can buy. Board of Trustees at the Ringling Museum in Sarasota, and all the high-profile committees and societies that she can handle. She's a very big contributor on the political scene. I think she's ready to call in a lot of favors."

"Her husband isn't even in his grave. Where's the concern, the compassion?"

"I don't know if there is any. My guess is that the marriage has been nothing more than a convenience and stepping-stone for a long time. Maybe forever. You know the congressman had been rumored to be playing around for years. He's up here, she's in Sarasota. Just last year they tried to tie him to that intern."

"Hell, everyone gets tied to an intern. It's the only way to get noticed."

Two nurses approached the table, hesitating for a moment. Sever knew the look. He put on a smile that he knew looked phony but it was the best he could muster. The shorter one in the baggy white pants made the first advance.

"You're on TV, right? I've seen you on MTV."

"People always confuse me with one of the Back Street Boys."

She giggled. "No, you know, you do the news sometimes about bands and stuff. Right?"

Sever glanced at Ginny, who sat back with a look of amusement on her face. She knew the game. Girls would flirt with him as if she wasn't even there. And the worst thing was, he always would flirt back. He knew it used to bother her. Now it seemed to amuse her. He nodded. "Sure."

"Wow. Do you have someone here? Is someone famous a patient?" She looked at her chubby blond friend, her eyes wide.

"I'm sorry. Nobody famous. Just an acquaintance."

"Oh, well, it was nice to meet you. What's your name?"

"Mick."

She hesitated, not knowing where to go with the conversation. He decided not to make it any easier and said nothing.

"Well, Mick, I'll wave at you the next time I see you on TV. 'Bye."

The two girls walked away, obviously having an animated conversation.

"You're a piece of work, Sever. I told you, some people never do change." She leaned across the table, looking into his face. "So, what's the next step? Time is wasting."

"I'm going to start with a background on the congressman. I'll try to be balanced, but, hey, this is my piece. I may vent some of my frustration in the article. In the meantime, if you're now officially on the payroll, how about trying to set up an interview with the lead detective. See when Chilli is being extradited, and see if I can talk to him. I was going to suggest an interview with Charlie White, the chauffeur, but that's out of the question. I'll touch base with T-Beau."

"Leaving someone out, aren't you?"

He closed his eyes for a second, trying to clear his mind from the outline he'd created. He kept them closed, focusing on the limo pulling away from the curb. Focus on the pain, the betrayal, and don't let the good times get in the way.

"Sure." He opened his eyes. "See if we can get an interview with Nicky Brand."

He put a ten on the table and they left the coffee shop. People in the hallway glanced at them as they walked by. Sever knew who they were watching. In her tight jeans and white turtleneck sweater, she was really something to see.

Chapter Fifteen

Alicia Shapply was staying the night, strictly for observation. The doctor said she had suffered physical and emotional trauma and he wanted to watch her until the following morning. Sever and Ginny grabbed a cab and headed for the hotel.

"May as well stay here. I can keep you in line."

"Good idea. I've got a king-size bed and—"

"You always try, don't you? I need my own room, Mick. It had better be in the budget."

Before the marriage, they'd been like rabbits, doing it every chance they got. During the marriage it was great for a while, until he started wandering again. And after the marriage broke up, it seemed they couldn't keep their hands off each other. But the last several times she'd turned him down cold. "Oh, it's in the budget, but it might be nice to remember how it used to be."

The cab pulled up in front of the hotel and the driver

deposited her two bags on the sidewalk. Sever picked them up and carried them inside the lobby. Matching soft leather bags monogrammed with "G.S." burned into the skin. He'd bought them for the honeymoon.

She touched his arm and he set the bags down. Shorter by a good five inches, she lightly held his shoulders and looked up into his eyes. He smelled the soft perfume. "I'm seeing someone. Don't make it tough, okay?"

For a moment he forgot to breathe. He could see the troubled look on her face, and he knew she was worried about him. He took in a deep breath. "Great. Serious?"

"I don't know. We're taking it as it comes. I don't want to talk about it with you right now. Why don't you get me a room? I want to get freshened up and get to work."

"Does he know you're here? With me?"

"He knows. He's not wild about the idea, but he knows. Get me the room, Sever. We've got work to do."

He went through the motions, checking the answering machine, pouring a Scotch, and flipping on the TV to see what was being reported about the limo driver. His press picture was all over the television. They hadn't wasted any time. The problem now was twofold. First, Ginny was seeing someone. Pissed him off. Second, it was tough to do a story when you were part of it. His objectivity had been compromised. He fished out Jamie Jordan's phone number in Georgetown and gave him a call.

"Jesus! Dude, you are all over the news. What did you get yourself into?"

"Jamie, settle down. You'll get your first installment in two days, maybe sooner. I'm going to do a background on the old man and his involvement in the entertainment industry. It seems like a good place to start, and I won't have to do a whole lot of research. And as a bonus, you get a firsthand account of the limo murder."

"I should ask, are you alright? Shit, that could have been you!"

"I'm fine. What happened just makes things easier. The people I've got to talk to already know I'm involved."

"So I can tell Ed and the guys that you'll produce in two days?"

"Count on it."

"And the piece today on the shooting? It's current and you were there, pal."

"I'll knock it off and e-mail it in the next hour."

Jordan chuckled on the other end. "Nobody's got a first-hand on this except us! That's about as good as you can get! I knew this was a good idea!"

Chapter Sixteen

The phone rang and he grabbed it. It seemed that his entire life revolved around hotel rooms, phones, and the laptop. What happened in between was just a prelude for the hotel room, phone, and his laptop.

"Mick, Chilli D will be in the D.C. jail about eight P.M. tonight. He didn't fight extradition."

"All right! And I can see him?"

"Not tonight. He and Nicky can only have visitors Monday and Thursday."

"What? The other days are holy days?"

"I don't know. They go by the alphabet—twelve P.M. to seven P.M. Monday and Thursday."

"Okay." He tried to gather his thoughts. Closing his eyes for a moment, he paused. "Ginny, this guy you're seeing . . ."

"We're not in high school anymore, Mick. Drop it. Don't bring it up again. Understood?"

He was quiet, chastised, and still pissed. The television

was now showing his picture, Robert Shapply's picture, Nicky Brand's picture, and Alicia Shapply's picture. He'd turned the sound down and he could only imagine what they were saying about the unholy foursome. The Fox News Washington bureau was really going overboard on this one.

"Eight P.M.?"

"Eight P.M. Do you want to be there?"

"I think so. I'll call T-Beau, we'll go down together."

"They'll have to arraign him. You're not going to get a conversation."

"And T-Beau doesn't get along with this attorney at all, so that angle won't work."

"He'll be in the D.C. jail tomorrow. We'll talk to him day after tomorrow. Don't get so impatient."

"We've both screwed this thing up."

She was quiet for a moment. "What thing? Oh. Will you please leave it alone?"

"I'd like to talk. We've got some unbelievable history, and it just feels like we should—"

"God damn it, Sever. I'll walk out on this project and I won't come back. Work with it. When I'm ready to talk to you, I will. You called me to do a job. If someone else can do that job, I'm out of here."

He watched the screen go dark for a second, then a commercial appeared with a circus clown riding a unicycle. He'd always wondered how you could do that. The solo balancing act seemed very tricky.

"No. You do it better than anyone. No more questions," he said.

"The funeral will be Monday morning. A very busy day." She took a deep breath. He could hear it. It almost sounded like she was taking a long drag on a cigarette. "Friends?" She had softened.

"Always."

"What? You're thinking of something."

"T-Beau. I was talking to him about Nick, and he said something about a man having only so many friends. And, if he starts losing them, he'd better start looking for some new ones. I don't want to lose you."

"I know. I know. We can stay friends, Mick. I think we can do that."

Chapter Seventeen

The limo piece was easy. He left out most of the conversation. He wasn't sure he understood it anyway. Her daughter and family fights, childhood friends, and passing on messages. It was all very strange, but the entire event reinforced his feeling about Mrs. Shapply. There was no warmth in that woman at all. The article would be straight, factual, with a slight editorial slant, leaving the interviews with the police to the newspaper staff. The soft hum of his laptop calmed him down.

Someone seems to want the Shapply family out of the way, and they're very serious about getting the job done. He briefly mentioned the hearings and the death of the congressman. *Today, I rode in the limousine with Mrs. Alicia Shapply, speaking with her about her late husband and her son.* There was no mention of the Ice Maiden's lack of emotion. He told the story as it happened, including her comment that her son was innocent, and sent it to Jordan. He felt certain they would lead with it in the morning. When he was done, he saved the story and opened a new file. This one would be much harder to write. There was a lot of personal involvement in the story of Robert Shapply and Nick Brand. Sever poured himself another Scotch. This time, he didn't add water.

At 11 P.M. he took a break, picked up the phone, and dialed room 220. The gravelly voice on the other end said, "Whasup?"

"Your boy came in tonight."

"And you din't call?"

"Nobody can see him until day after tomorrow. Strict visitation rules."

"Shit! I'll call Freddy. We'll get in early."

"I thought you didn't get along with Freddy."

"I'm the Love Doctor. I get along with anybody if I want to."

"If you arrange it, call me."

"Mick, if I work this out with Freddy, we need to talk to Chill and get the complete story. Stay by the phone. I'll be back to you soon." The line went dead.

He thought about calling Ginny's room. She could be working late, poring over someone's writing, helping them make it come alive, giving it focus and what she called "punch." Maybe she was watching TV or maybe she'd already gone to bed. In their younger days they could party all night—hours and hours sometimes. Some uppers, some alcohol, and the right crowd, and nobody crashed for three days running. A lot of wild things happened in those days.

Instead, he went back to the laptop. He made a stab at explaining the investments that Shapply and his stepson had been involved with. After all these years it was still a murky situation, one that had never been fully explained. Sever and a handful of A-list clients had their earnings invested in a holding company that held majority positions in trendy real estate, oil companies, and some questionable investments in the Caribbean and West Indies. The positions were high risk, and apparently Shapply and Brand were making commissions not only from the A-list clients, but from the holding company as well, double-dipping and making out like bandits. When the holding company folded, Sever and his partners lost everything, while the congressman and his stepson walked away with more money than God. Almost everyone suspected some shady dealings, but no one could prove it. And now, Shapply was a congressman, or had been until his murder. And Nicky Brand was still in the business of handling financial affairs for entertainers. You could fool some of the people all of the time.

At 11:45, T-Beau called. "There's no way we can see him early. Got to be the regular time. They got him buttoned up tighter than a suit. What do you hear about the funeral?"

"The funeral is at ten A.M. and visiting hours are from twelve to seven. I thought I'd be at the jail at twelve sharp. I want to see Chilli as soon as possible."

"And what about Nicky?"

"I'll see him."

"Mick, you gonna be okay? People shootin' at you and shit?"

"I'm fine. I don't think anybody is after me, but I've got to watch out who I hang with."

"Aw, Mick, the only people after me are a handful of angry husbands. The wives got a taste of the Love Doctor and don't wanna go back."

Sever went back to his computer but his heart wasn't in it. He flipped the TV on and fell asleep before the first commercial. As he drifted into his sleep pattern he saw the look in Alicia Shapply's eyes as the car swerved into the median. She was cool, calm, the Ice Maiden. The initial shock hadn't seemed to phase her at all.

Chapter Eighteen

You know, you'll always know, 'cause I'm showing you with every breath that I take. And you know, baby, you'll always know, I'll prove it to you every move that I make . . . make you happy, content, that's always the way that I meant it to be. Always. Always.

Soothing. The Love Doctor. It was like someone from the forties hearing Sinatra or Martin. This music got under your skin. And of course T-Beau's songs were popular just about the time he started his relationship with Ginny. Romance and relationships had everything to do with the way he felt about this music.

He slipped the CD out of his computer and pushed in Oddman, a new rapper who was on the list to be chastised, criticized, and ostracized by the Shapply committee. The harsh scratchy percussion jangled his nerves and the tricky lyrics tumbled out of the man's mouth. His lyrics were a little clearer than the average hip-hop message:

> *I don't know if Daddy did his little girl or mommy drowned the baby. Or lickety-split the brother had a time with Sister Sadie. Fuckin' family problems fuck up more than this one nigger and I wouldn't put it past the reason pullin' on this trigger. Pull the trigger shoot the bitch pay her back all right, gonna be a player later on tonight. If you got the balls to do it blow it all away. If you're gonna be a player, better learn to play.*

Sever shut it down and closed his eyes. In most cases he defended it. There would always be the question, does art reflect life or does life reflect art? Shit, it *was* his problem. He'd set himself up as the scribe of rock and roll. Critics referred to him as the dean of the genre. And if you're the dean, you've got to take a stand. So his stand had come to this. When you allowed anyone to censor any form of art, you gave away your freedom. Still, there were times when he secretly wished a Shapply-type hearing would put some fear into some of these artists and some of their record companies . . . tone them down a notch. He opened the jewel case with the latest CD from Chilli D. Chilli had produced this himself, just before T-Beau picked him up.

The lyrics were fast and tricky, like he was taking lessons from Eminem. Triplets and tongue rolls, and although Sever couldn't pick up all the words, he got the message. The same tired story of a black man who lived the life, walked the walk, talked the talk, and all that. And if you wanted the good life, be cool and don't take any shit from anyone and you'll have women falling all over you and boys from the 'hood watching your back and . . . and he took it out of his laptop. There was a lot of good, innovative hip-hop, even some really good gangsta rap that he admired. This wasn't it.

He picked up the phone and called T-Beau's room, leaving a message on the hotel machine. "Beau. Stop by the room. I need to pick your brain."

T-Beau called back five minutes later.

Sever sipped a beer, T-Beau a soda, and Ginny an iced tea. They watched the eclectic group of people who poured into the Union Station restaurant with its microbrewery assortment of overpriced beers. There were Capitol Hill folk in their suits with official-looking plastic name tags around their necks, tourists still dressed in summerwear with the late October temperatures in the mid-seventies, news people, from Fox, C-Span, and MSNBC right next door, and locals who were looking for a quick lunch.

"I remember the gold Harley," Ginny said. "The first time Mick and I saw you, you came roaring out on stage. Still got it?"

T-Beau laughed. "Still got Glitter."

"You named it?"

"I name 'em all. Fifteen in the collection. Triumphs, Harleys. I got a 1939 Indian Chief with a sidecar. Call him Tonto." He glanced around the busy room, then in a hushed tone said, "I got Chill a bike when he agreed to sign with my management company. We named his Bad Rap."

Sever nodded. "I hope that's what this is, a Bad Rap."

"Speaking of that, there's a couple of things I need to do.

I want to look further into this Reverend Joseph Evans connection." Ginny took another sip of her iced tea, extra sugar and extra lemon. It made Sever's mouth pucker. "You guys are going to see Chilli tomorrow and, of course . . ." she trailed off. They all knew who else Mick would see. "Apparently Reverend Evans and Alicia Shapply plan on pursuing the hearings. I'd like to know more about their involvement."

"Somethin' that's strange? Charlie White's involvement." T-Beau rested his big arms on the table and folded his hands as if ready to make a solemn announcement. "Charlie drops off the congressman and the congressman is killed. Shot dead. Charlie drives the congressman's wife and *he* is killed. Shot dead. Odds are pretty slim on that one. You think maybe Charlie White had somethin' to do with it? Maybe he set up the congressman, then somebody shot him to keep him quiet?"

Sever nodded. "Charlie White could control the congressman's whereabouts. He might have set him up."

"That's another area I need to look into. I'll run a background check on White, see what the police know, or what they'll tell me. I should be able to get enough material this afternoon and tomorrow to at least give you a day or two worth of work." Ginny excused herself, pushed back her chair, and headed for the restroom. T-Beau watched in admiration as she walked away, her blond hair pulled back carelessly in a clip and her form-fitting jeans hugging her tight rear.

"Check it out. You had some fine tail there."

Sever smiled. If he didn't know the Love Doctor so well he might have been offended. As it was, he took it as a serious compliment. "*Had* is the word, Beau. There's been mention of someone else who may or may not be serious."

"Trouble with us, bro', we get a lot of strange, but what we really want is what we cannot have. Makes it sweeter than candy, you know what I'm sayin'?"

This time Sever knew exactly what he was saying.

"Just a law of nature. You and me, we want it the worst way, but if we get it, we gonna end up treatin' it like shit. Better for all concerned we don't get it at all."

"I'm sure you did a song about that somewhere in your illustrious career."

"I'm not sure I ever did, but shit, it would make a good one. Comin' from the Doctor and all. Somethin' like 'I only want what I can't have and baby I can't have you.' "

Sever nodded. "But if I get you to myself, you won't believe what I'll put you through."

"Dawg!" T-Beau shouted out. The people at the next table looked up, startled. "I may just have to go back into the studio. That's got the makin' of a serious song."

"We'll have to add some gunplay and a couple of 'fuck yous' to make sure it gets airplay."

"Aw, Mick. You gonna get on a roll about hip-hop?"

"You're working that end now. Producing people like Chilli. You tell me. What makes it so . . . so enticing?"

"You know. What I tell you ain't any different than what you now already."

"Give me your rendition. Do you buy into it?"

"Wouldn't produce it if I din't."

"Okay."

"Put it in the white boys' perspective. You dug the Beach Boys. Shit, all you white dudes dug the Beach Boys. Singin' 'bout sun, surf, sand, hot cars, and hotter women. Now, Mick, they was singin' about culture. From where they sat, out in

California, this shit was happenin' all around them. Nothin' unusual 'bout that."

"You're right." Sever took a deep swallow of the bitter beer. "I know where this is going."

"Sure you do. Niggah sits up in Detroit, or in L.A. or New York surrounded by gang bangers, whores, thieves, and killers. He writes a song, usin' the language he hears on the street every day. He's writin' 'bout culture. What's happenin' on the street. Now, the way I see it, he's got as much right to sing about his culture as your lily-white Beach Boys got to sing about theirs."

"Surfing, fast women, and cars. It wasn't a cry to go out and kill someone or beat women or—"

"Mick, it's culture. Man, you're a writer. What do they tell every writer? Write what you know. Chill got beat up by the Man. So he writes about revenge. It's what he knows, what he feels. Write what you know."

Sever listened. It was simple and it was true, but what T-Beau was saying was the basis for his article. There was no need to make it more complicated than it was.

"When I started writin' love songs? When I was tellin' all the women of the world that I would worship and protect them and treat them like a goddess? Shit, Mick, I was a big, homely guy who couldn't get to first base with a woman. So here I was, imaginin' how I would treat the first girl who would commit to me. I knew that when some fine lady said, 'Beau, you and me are gonna make beautiful music together,' that I would worship, protect, and treat her like a goddess. I wrote about not only what I thought I knew, but what I imagined. Ain't nothin' wrong with that."

"So when some of these wanna-be players write about the gangster life . . ."

"They're writin' 'bout how they imagine it's gonna be. Then they write about how it is. And some of them, like Hammer, remember him? Well, when it's over, the MC Hammers write about how it *was*." He chuckled. "Hammer. Man, that dude fucked himself up so bad. He lost it all. Anyway, that's what you do, Mick. You talk about what you know or what you imagine. I don't have to tell you." He finished his soda, caught the eye of the waitress as she bustled by, dropped his voice an octave, and asked for the check.

"You ask for the check like you're trying to seduce her." Sever laughed out loud.

"Always askin' for the order, Mick. Always. Always."

Ginny walked back, coming to a stop at the table. She gazed at both of them with a sly smile on her face. "Something happened. In that brief time I was gone, it looks like you two may have solved the world's problems."

T-Beau dropped his voice again, giving her a big grin. "We may have started some new ones, baby."

They made plans to meet the following morning. The funeral for a murdered United States congressman promised to attract nationwide attention, and Sever wanted to see just who showed up.

Chapter Nineteen

Federal marshals checked every I.D. Terrorism being what it was, and the murdered body of a high-profile congressman lying in state, they were taking no chances. Ginny handed her driver's license over, and Sever saw the brief glance from the marshal.

"Virginia Sever?" He handed back the license. Still Sever. What once had been his.

T-Beau stepped up and handed his to the same marshal.

"Tony Beauregard?" The marshal smiled. "Wow. I always wondered where you got T-Beau. My dad loves your music."

T-Beau turned to Sever. "Ever feel older than dirt?"

Sever followed suit and they walked into the gigantic cathedral together. A commotion behind them announced the arrival of the vice president. His entourage of Secret Service, assistants, and several other senators and congressmen surrounded him, but Sever knew who it was.

From the outside, the cathedral resembled a medieval castle, and the inside had the same rather cold charm. Glaring gargoyles and carved angels stared out from the walls, over two hundred stained-glass windows filtered the multicolored sunlight, and statues of famous American figures stood at every turn.

"Woodrow Wilson is buried here." Sever's eyes wandered over the hundreds of opulent bouquets lining the aisles and the altar with all the colors of the rainbow. The brass casket was almost hidden with chrysanthemums, roses, and carnations. Living green foliage spilled from expensive wicker baskets and copper urns. Even the carved saints at the altar seemed in awe of the abundance of floral creations.

The lobbyists and favor-seekers who had paid for a lot of the foliage today weren't going to get any more favors from Bob Shapply.

T-Beau sniffed the air. "Smells like . . . like . . ."

"A funeral?"

"Yeah. That's what it is."

They took their seats in the spacious room, Sever letting his eyes scan the several thousand mourners. The widow sat aisle seat front and center. Not surprisingly, she appeared calm and dignified. Cool as ice.

And beside her, hands folded in front, sat his boyhood buddy, Nicky Brand. The N kid. M and N forever. Handcuffs were probably locked securely around his wrists and the two gentlemen beside him were cops for sure. Brand kept his eyes focused during the entire service, never looking at anyone or anything that wasn't directly in front of him. The service was typical. A brass quartet played a Bach concerto and a Presbyterian minister gave the message. *A man's good works live after him.* Sever thought he could have used a better speech writer. Then three members of the house got up, one after another, and talked about the courage that Shapply had shown in so many areas of his public life. Sever thought about the cowardliness he'd shown in his private life.

He nudged T-Beau as soon as the eulogies had been given and they slipped out. They wanted to see Chilli D as soon as possible. Nicky Brand was going to be a while. He was attending church with his mother and that obviously hadn't happened for a long, long time.

Chapter Twenty

They stepped out into the cool October air, the pale blue sky overhead flecked with thin white clouds. Limousines lined the street, and taxicabs were clustered up ahead. Sever glanced at T-Beau, strangely quiet now and head bent down as if he was studying his large feet, as they walked down the sidewalk to the cabs.

"You okay, Beau?"

"Yeah. Just thinkin'." The man raised his head and briefly glanced over his shoulder.

Limo drivers leaned against the long sleek Lincolns and Cadillacs, talking to each other in hushed tones, or they sat in their cars reading magazines, doing crossword puzzles, or checking their dwindling stock portfolios, oblivious to the funeral inside. A couple were on cell phones, waiting for their charges to finish with their condolences.

The two men who fell in behind them were moving fast. Sever hadn't noticed them until he heard the heavy footsteps.

He quickened the pace. T-Beau gave another fast look over his shoulder and followed Sever's lead. The line of taxis was half a block up, and Sever considered jogging. There was something threatening about the quick steps behind him.

The man was on his heels, almost literally. Sever motioned to T-Beau with a nod of his head and they turned right, following the side road instead of walking toward the taxis. The move was sudden and Sever expected the two men to continue walking straight ahead. He heard their breathing, short gasps of breath, probably smokers. Sever was almost running. His legs worked hard and fast like they were pistons as he tried to distance himself from the men behind. He could feel the strain on his knee. T-Beau seemed short on breath, too, keeping up as he leaned forward, using all that weight for momentum.

This was a mistake. He should have kept on the main road. No security here, no limo drivers, just a row of cars double-parked on the far side of the street.

Sever spun around and stopped, freezing in place. He'd learned in boxing to do something they don't expect. It can give you valuable seconds. But you'd better use those seconds wisely.

T-Beau hadn't caught the signal and took another four or five steps. The two men behind them looked confused. They'd stopped, catching their breath. One had a buzz cut and wore a trench coat, and the other seemed stuffed into an ill-fitting gray sport coat, his black hair greased back. His dark eyes were set deep in his pock-marked face as they stared at Sever. In a fraction of a second Sever saw a hand come out of the tan trench coat, a small black pistol clenched tightly in the man's fist. Buzz Cut raised the pistol and slashed at Sever's head.

T-Beau moved fast for a big man, chopping down on the gun arm as the man screamed in pain.

"No guns, you motherfucker—"

The second man kicked high, catching the black singer in the chest and sending him tumbling back off the sidewalk onto the street. He lay dazed as the driver of a white Lexus hit the brakes, his car screeching and swerving to the curb, missing the big man by inches. The driver swung open his door and ran into the street, leaning down to see if T-Beau was all right.

Sever spun around, throwing a quick punch at the kicker, hitting him solidly on the jaw, his head snapping back. The old one-two. Sever hit him with the second punch in his midsection as the man bent over in agony, struggling to stay erect. The boxing lessons had paid off again. The man with the buzz cut and trench coat glanced back toward the main road, then scooped up the dropped gun and grabbed his partner by the arm, pulling him away as they moved quickly down the sidewalk toward the taxis.

All the security just a block away and not a cop anywhere when you needed one. Sever briefly watched them go, then ran into the street and helped T-Beau to his feet. They stumbled to the sidewalk.

"Jesus Christ, you could have been killed!"

"It may be that Jesus Christ saved him."

Sever turned and looked hard at the man who spoke. Standing there in an expensive gray wool suit, an off-white shirt, and a blue raw silk tie knotted perfectly, he was somewhat smaller than he appeared on television.

"Is there anything I can do?" The man reached out and took Sever's hand. "I know you, but I don't think we've ever met. I'm Nick Brand's uncle, Joseph Evans."

Chapter Twenty-one

It was Sever's second limo ride since arriving in the capital city.

"We can drop you off at your hotel, or anywhere else you're going." Evans smiled at Sever. "It's really good to finally meet you. Your name has come up a lot in family discussions."

Sever rubbed his bruised knuckles. "I'm glad you came along when you did. I don't know how long those two would have stuck around."

"I wanted to meet you. I saw you and your friend"—he motioned to T-Beau—"walking out and I thought I'd catch up with you. I'm glad you're both alright.

"Didn't seem like a robbery." T-Beau nursed a sore rib. "It looked like somebody was . . ." he hesitated.

"What?" Sever asked.

"I don't know. I was just thinking, you were in that limo when the chauffeur took a bullet, now this."

"Somebody's out to get me?"

"Just a thought." T-Beau seemed to sulk in the corner of the limousine.

"You're safe. The Lord was with you. A gathering of angels." Evans again gave Sever a warm smile. "It's a sad day." Evans changed the conversation. "Bob was a marvelous man. Oh, I know what your relationship was with him, but, Mick, he was a changed person. What happened in his past was in the past. This man had made a miraculous transformation."

Sever nodded, not believing a word of it. There certainly hadn't been any financial reimbursement for the money Shapply and his son stole.

"He repented. And after the hearings, he was going to approach Nick. Right now, Nick thinks that we're the enemy, trying to bring down his clients. Bob feels, or felt, that Nick would see the bigger picture after the hearings."

"I understand you had a lot to do with Robert Shapply's change of heart."

"The Lord had a lot to do with Bob Shapply's change of heart. If I can bring a man to the Lord, then I give all the glory to the Lord." He laughed. "I don't mean to sound like a TV evangelist, Mick. Believe me, I'm not in the pulpit all the time, but I do believe that Bob Shapply had a true transformation, and he had a lot to repent!"

"Mrs. Shapply mentioned that the congressman had issues with his daughter. She wanted me to intercede with Nick and ask him to talk to Amber. Do you know anything about that?"

"Barbados was a long time ago, Mick."

"Barbados?"

"Oh. I assumed you were talking about their falling out when she was thirteen! You see, they haven't really . . . well, it's an involved story, but it's a family matter. I don't think my sister should ask you to involve yourself."

The limo pulled up to the curb and the driver hopped out and opened their doors.

"Thanks for the ride, Mr. Evans."

"Please, call me Joseph."

"I'll do it. Thanks again."

They walked into the hotel, T-Beau still quiet. "Beau, are you up for this? The interview? You took a hell of a kick out there."

"Sure. Let me get cleaned up and we'll meet down here in fifteen." The big man walked slowly to the elevator, never looking at Sever.

Chapter Twenty-two

Sever took off the sport coat, untied the tie, and stripped off the shirt and pants. He put on a comfortable blue cotton shirt, rolled the sleeves once, then slipped on a pair of jeans. He splashed water on his face and checked the phone for messages. There were none. He punched in Ginny's room number, but the message service picked up. He decided to tell her about today in person and hung up the phone.

He took the elevator down to two, and took a left, heading toward 202. As he rounded the corner he saw the man walking at the far end of the hall. Although his back was to Sever he looked familiar. Buzz cut and a tan trench coat. The man's hands were thrust into his pockets as he turned the corner. Sever sprinted down the hallway, dodging a maid and her cleaning cart as she emerged from one of the rooms. By the time he reached the corner, there was no sign of the man. It had to be a coincidence. He was just a little gun-shy, that was all. No need to panic. He retraced his steps. When he got to

202, he hesitated. It was the exact spot he'd first seen the man walking away.

Sever knocked on the door. He could hear T-Beau's deep loud voice inside. "I told you, we'll deal with it later."

"Beau! It's me."

The door opened slowly.

"Hey, Mick. I was . . ."

"On the phone?"

"Yeah. Go down to the lobby. I told you I'd meet you there. Let me finish up here and we'll grab a cab and go see Chill."

His voice was icy.

Sever walked back to the corner, gazing down the long hallway. Whoever had been there was long gone.

Chapter Twenty-three

He wore a bright orange uniform. It could have been a stage costume for one of his concerts or an outfit he would wear on a video. On Chilli D it looked stylish. He pulled up a chair and picked up the phone. T-Beau spoke into the mouthpiece on the other side of the glass.

" 'Sup, my man?"

"Hey, Beau. I'm a little stressed."

"Write a song. Got to use what is handed you. Make the experience pay!"

"Yeah. I'll write a song like 'Prison Is a Stone Cold Bitch.' "

"Got a ring to it. Get down to business 'cause we ain't got a lot of time. Mick Sever here is workin' on the story."

"Yeah. My lawyer says I got to keep my mouth shut. Hard for me to do, Beau."

"Won't be nothin' printed you don't want printed, am I right, Mick?"

Chilli D shifted his eyes, watching an inmate down the row who was talking to his mother.

"Chill?"

"Whatch you wanna know?"

"They found a gun or somethin'?"

"Got to keep quiet. Can't trust nobody. People are out to get me."

"Talk to me, Chill. I told Mick here that you'd communicate. Help yourself."

"Nothin' to say. To either of you."

Sever spoke into his phone. "Chilli, I'm not here to nail the lid on your coffin. I want to find out what happened. Let me help. I promise you, I'm not out to get anyone."

He gave Sever a long look. "Yeah. They found a gun."

"*The* gun?"

"That's what they're sayin'."

"Where?"

"My pad."

"How?"

"If I knew, you'd be the first one I'd tell. But I don't."

"You came into Washington the day the congressman was killed and left the next."

"Yeah."

"Why?"

Chilli's eyes drifted again, down the row of prisoners talking to relatives, friends, and lovers.

"Why, Chilli?"

"Had a meeting with Nick."

"Who's also implicated."

"That's what I heard."

"Chilli, you're not helping much."

"No matter what I say, I just dig myself deeper."

"What was the meeting about?"

"Robert Shapply, his dad."

"And?"

"And about the money I owed Nick. I took out a personal loan, you know what I'm sayin'?"

"You discussed the hearings?"

"Yeah."

"What else?" Sever stared through the glass, looking into the eyes of the rap star.

"Killin' his old man."

"You discussed killing Robert Shapply?" Sever felt a shiver go through his body.

T-Beau shouted into his mouthpiece. "You shut the fuck up. What the hell are you sayin'?"

"You told me, tell it and we won't print it all." He was frustrated. "The truth, Beau. That's what we talked about. How this whole mess would quiet down if the old man was dead. Now you see my predicament? Man, if Nicky, the *white* boy, tells them about the money and tells them we discussed killin' old man Shapply, then I don't have a prayer."

T-Beau breathed deeply. "You already been down once, bro'. Two murder convictions ain't gonna look too good on your résumé."

"Yeah."

Sever spoke. "Did you kill the congressman?"

"No. Never did it. It was just big talk. 'What if' kind of stuff."

"And Nick didn't do it either?"

"I can't speak to that. Nick has done all right by me, but . . ."

"But what?"

"I suppose someone under pressure might do just about anything."

Sever glanced at T-Beau, then back to Chilli. "Are you speaking from experience?"

"I didn't kill him. Do you hear me? Nick was worried that the old man was going to do damage to his customer base. That's all I can say."

They were quiet for a moment.

"Chill, I'm gonna do some searching, ask some questions."

"I know, Beau. I got friends on the outside. Ain't nobody just standin' around. Things are happenin'."

Sever watched the rapper hang up the phone. Chilli D reached out his hand and pressed it flat against the glass separating them. T-Beau did the same, covering the hand on the reverse side of the clear separating wall. They stared into each other's eyes. As if on cue they both took their hands from the window and separated, neither looking back. Sever and T-Beau walked to the door and the guard let them out.

Chapter Twenty-four

"Chill didn't do it!" T-Beau seemed defiant.

They stood on the sidewalk, the sun warming them in the chilled air.

"Show me a killer who admits his crime."

"I'm tellin' you, Mick. I know my boy. Chill and me are close. The boy wouldn't lie to me. Somebody is tryin' to set him up, and that's the truth."

"What makes you so sure?"

"Gut instinct. And somebody is tryin' to get you off this story."

"Where do you get that?"

"Number one, Charlie White takes a bullet in the limo. That bullet was meant for you. Somebody tryin' to get you to back off the story."

"No reason to believe it was meant for me."

"Number two, you get attacked outside the cathedral for no reason. Somebody tryin' to get you off the case."

"I seem to remember you were there, too. Maybe they were after you."

"You know better. There's no reason to come after me."

Sever decided not to pursue the answer. "And the reason they want to get me off the case?"

"It just makes sense. The cops got Chilli, and they got Nick. They seem to be happy with those two. Case closed. But you, you keep pokin' around, lookin' for *another* suspect. Somebody wants you to leave well enough alone. You might find the real killer, and they don't want that."

"That's where you're wrong, Beau. When it comes to Chilli, I think the evidence sounds overwhelming."

"I don't buy it."

Sever was quiet, mulling it over in his head. Maybe someone was trying to get his attention. But Buzz Cut in the trench coat had been seen coming out of T-Beau's room, or damned close to it, and he needed an explanation for that. He decided now was not the time to ask.

"What was that he said about 'Nobody is just standing around. Things are happening'?"

"Chilli's got friends. That's all, Mick! Chill didn't do the crime. Didn't. Somebody's got to be in his corner. He knows people. And chances are, Nick Brand didn't do the deed either. So it's up to us on the outside. That's all."

"Up to us? It's a story, Beau. That's all it is. The story is that Chilli is a killer and they found the gun. It sounds pretty cut and dried."

T-Beau frowned. "You're wrong, Mick. You're just wrong."

"I've got to be back in about an hour to find out if Nick will see me. Want to grab a sandwich somewhere?"

"Naw. I'm catchin' a cab and headin' back to the hotel. You got to be alone with yourself, get your head in the right place."

Sever nodded. He wasn't sure where that was right now, but it seemed to make sense. He found a coffee shop three blocks away and grabbed a copy of the *Washington Post* to help pass the time. The stories ran together and didn't seem to make much sense, and an hour went by much too quickly.

Chapter Twenty-five

In the brief moment between consciousness and sleep, he often saw glimmers of truth. They were magical moments, with a hint of his past, or a glimpse of his future. There were times when the moment revealed a thought buried deep inside his subconscious, and the impact would rouse him from his relaxed state. The moment was a blessing and a curse, and he had absolutely no control over what would happen in that brief moment in time. Last night he'd had a brief, lucid moment. He saw Nicky Brand, smiling at him, saying "Friends forever, Mick." And he'd meant it. Sever knew he'd meant it. And knowing firsthand what had happened, it made it that much more difficult to walk back to the D.C. jail and do what needed to be done.

He called the hotel from a pay phone. It was harder and harder to find one now that 99 percent of the population seemed to own a cell phone. Ginny hadn't come back. He could use her cheerful voice right about now. He needed to debrief. Thousands of interviews, with every type of personality possible—he dreaded this one more than any other. He walked into the building and signed the necessary papers. He'd finally made the move, now it remained to be seen if Nick would follow suit.

The uniformed officer ushered him into the same room he'd been in an hour ago with the glass partition. Several women sat on chairs making small talk to inmates on the other side. One young white girl held a small baby in her arms, looking down at the child and never at the man on the other side. Hell of a way to introduce a kid to his father. There was no sign of Nicky Brand. Sever glanced at his watch, wondering where Ginny was. Probably doing some background on Charlie White. He hoped she could get access to the police interview with the chauffeur. Supposedly White had been the last one to see Bob Shapply alive. The last person except the killer.

"Hey, bro'. Long time no see."

He glanced up. The clear blue eyes, high cheekbones, the tossled hair, and the perfect smile. Nicky Brand, looking as calm and confident as ever. The years evaporated, if only for a moment, and the M and N boys were back together.

"I didn't know if you'd take the call."

"Hell, I didn't think you'd call."

They looked each other over, the silence somewhat embarrassing.

"Orange. Not your best color."

"Won't be for long. I had nothing to do with this. You know, I didn't approve of the man. Lots of things I didn't like about him. Like what happened to you, but I didn't have him killed."

There it was. Short, brief, on the table. Didn't pay someone to kill his stepdad, and didn't approve of how Sever had been treated. It all seemed so simple. And there was that shallow desire to put all of it behind them and accept the apology, if that's what it was. But the deep hurt remained. It couldn't be that simple. It wouldn't be that simple.

"I talked to your mom."

"Ice Maiden. Isn't she something?"

"Did you talk to her on the way to the funeral?"

"Hell, no. She got the judge to let me go to the church and we sat together. That was it, man, and that was as close as we've been in years. You know the story. She couldn't care less about her kids."

More silence.

"How's Ginny?"

"Good. She's here."

"You two. Should have made it work." Nick shook his head.

"What happened?"

"With me and Ginny?" Brand gave him a sly grin.

"Jesus. Don't tell me . . ."

"Mick. I was kidding. What do you want to know? What happened with me and the congressman way back when, or what's happening right now?" Brand held the quizzical smile on his face.

"Maybe both."

"That's a long story. I suppose we should talk about it after I get out of here. This"—he spread his hands as if to showcase the small interview room he was in—"this I can't explain. Supposedly Chilli implicated me. Now, he and I both know that I had nothing to do with killing the old man."

"Chili says he's afraid *you're* going to implicate *him*. He said the two of you talked about the congressman the day he was killed."

"Oh shit. Is that what some of this is about? Damn! Something might have been said, like, this would all go away if the old man wasn't pushing it so hard. Chilli was afraid for his career."

"And your $250,000 loan to Chilli depended on his career."

"You've been doing your homework. I see your point. But trust me, amigo, I could never kill someone for $250,000. Besides, he would have paid that back with his signing bonus." Brand paused. "Mick, I couldn't kill someone. You know that."

He didn't know that. Not anymore.

"The cops told me that they don't put someone in here unless they're pretty sure that person is not getting out."

"Alright, I'm concerned. You may not think much of me after, well, you know. However, you know I'm not a killer. And I wouldn't pay someone to do it for me."

"I don't know you at all."

"Yeah, you do. You know me better than anyone. You don't believe that now, but it's true. Someday we'll have that talk and you'll see it's just me. The same Nick. M and N, bro'."

Sever didn't respond. Maybe it was the underlying fear of being in prison, but Nick was just a little too slick. There were a thousand questions and he couldn't ask one of them.

"Mick, if Chilli killed the old man, someone put him up to it and it wasn't me. I don't think he'd have killed the old man on his own. He's not the kind of guy who takes the lead."

The young girl with the baby brushed by Sever. He glanced up and saw her wiping away the tears in her eyes.

"Who would set him up?"

"Hell, could have been anyone upset with the old man. And there were a bunch of people. Could have been you."

Sever fought to keep his cool.

"I'm sorry. That wasn't fair. Hell, you probably had a right to think about it. Killing me *and* the old guy. There's a bunch of people who are going to take a hit from these hearings. Chilli is one of them. Could have been someone from Rapsta Records."

"I thought about killing both of you. We'll deal with that later."

Brand smiled. The boyish good looks, the bright eyes, nothing seemed to diminish the charm of Nicky Brand.

"Rapsta Records, that's the company that's recording Chilli?"

"Will be when T-Beau gets him signed."

"And then you get your money back, the $250,000?"

Brand ignored it. "I've got confidence in T-Beau. He's not a client, but he's got a lot of savvy about artists. If he backs somebody, it's a first-class investment and he's backing Chilli big time."

"And the story is that you told Chilli to kill the congressman and you'd forgive the loan."

"I loaned him the money, Mick. It was a solid investment with interest and everything. I didn't offer to forgive the loan. That's the long and the short of it."

"Alright, let me change the subject. I had a talk with your mother."

"I saw it on the TV. Man, you were lucky you didn't buy the farm."

"She had this secret rendezvous to ask me to talk to you."

Brand stared at Sever, the question in his expression.

"She says you'll be okay. They can't hold you because you didn't do it. However, she wants me to tell you to intercede with Amber. It seems Amber wants to contest the will or something."

Brand seemed genuinely confused. "She wants me to talk to Amber? About what?"

"It wasn't clear. We were, uh, interrupted before we could finish the conversation."

Behind Brand, an armed guard walked along the row of prisoners, glancing at the round black clock on the wall. Sever remembered classrooms where he and Nicky watched the same industrial-looking clocks, waiting for the bell so they could get the hell out and raise a little hell.

"She thinks Amber is going to muddy the water. She wants you to tell Amber to stay out of it. I thought maybe you could shed some light on the subject."

Brand was quiet. The light in his eyes seemed to dim. His shoulders slumped and the brilliant orange of his suit suddenly contrasted with his skin, making him look pale and fragile.

"There was never a real bond between father and daughter. When she was twelve or thirteen she lost a friend—"

"Margarite. Named her daughter after her."

"Yeah. Mom and Robert went to Barbados. Robert had invested in a recording company over there, and he represented a couple of calypso acts. It seemed like a great way to take a vacation and write it off. They took Amber and Margarite and while they were there . . ." he trailed off.

"The girl was killed."

"That's right. They never found the killer and Amber's never been the same. She grew distant from Mom, and

Robert, and never forgave them for taking the vacation. Of course, the girl's parents never forgave them either. Yeah, I can see her still pining for Margarite."

The guard passed back the other way. He tapped Brand on the back with his hand.

"Ten minutes."

Nicky nodded and looked at Sever with pleading eyes. "I've got a first-class attorney. I've got enough money to post about any bail, but what I need on the other side is someone I know."

"Does Chilli have some outside contacts?"

"Like anyone in that business, he's got his so-called posse. Bodyguards, a dozen guys who just hang around, four or five women, and of course everyone is on the payroll. If this murder rap hangs on much longer, that posse won't."

Sever nodded. "I'm working the story, Nick."

"I need a friend, Mick."

"Our friendship died a long time ago."

"Then follow the leads. You could be the one chance to get me out, bro'. Find out who did it and why. I'm telling you, I didn't do it. Swear on Elvis's grave, man."

"On Elvis's grave?"

"Swear. Remember? There was nothing more solemn."

Sever stood up.

"That's an oath we never took lightly, Mick. Maybe when this whole thing blows over we can take that trip again. Shit, that was some trip. Remember? Graceland, here we come!"

"Yeah. Graceland. Memphis, Tennessee."

"Mick, the Ice Maiden didn't take you out just for a joy ride. There's something in this convoluted mess that involves Amber. Talk to her."

"You think it has something to do with you being in here?"

"I think if my mother brought it up, it has something to do with the situation in which she finds herself. If the Ice Maiden is nothing else, she's very self-serving. If Amber is making some waves and my mother wants her to stop, she'll find a way to shut her up. Mick, talk to Amber. She's still in Sarasota."

"I'll look into it." He hung up the phone and turned from the glass. Taking two steps, he looked back and saw Brand still sitting there, watching. He'd pressed his hand to the glass.

Brand mouthed the words. "Elvis's grave."

Sever nodded. The King was dead. Long live the King.

Chapter Twenty-six

He picked up a copy of the *Washington Times* in the busy hotel lobby. The front page announced the funeral and tomorrow's edition would probably give it a review. A sidebar announced that black activist Louis Farrakhan had just held a press conference, asking rappers to soften their message. Everyone was jumping on the bandwagon.

The line to her room was busy. He finally walked down the hall and knocked on the door. It took her a minute but she answered and motioned him inside. She picked up the receiver and resumed a conversation.

"Sure. Well, Mick just walked in so it's time he and I debrief. Un-huh. Me, too. Right. I'll see you in three or four days. Un-huh. I'm sure. I told you, me, too."

He saw the look in her eyes and it bothered him. She missed the guy. She used to have that look when she talked to him, until he'd fucked it all up. Or maybe they both fucked it up. This looked pretty serious to him.

She hung up and turned to him, brushing her hair back behind her ears. “So, I’ve been thinking about you. Was it as bad as you thought it would be?”

She walked to the minibar and took out a bottle of Dewars. Opening it, she poured half in one glass and half in another. She ran tap water into the glasses and handed Sever one. “You look like you could use this.”

He let his eyes caress her, a soft brown cotton blouse, loose at the collar and just a hint of cleavage, and corduroy pants that hugged her curves. She’d kicked off the shoes, and when she sat down on the bed she tucked her bare feet underneath her. He wanted the years to roll back, but they didn’t.

“A couple of things happened before I talked to Nick.” He pulled up the desk chair and straddled it backwards. “Let me tell you about my day.”

When he was finished, she let out a sigh. “It’s one catastrophe after another. Who do you think set it up?”

“You won’t believe it if I tell you.”

“Try me.”

“Not yet.”

“Why not?”

“This one I’ve got to work out on my own. For now, that’s what happened.”

She stared into space. “Maybe you should forget about this story?”

“I can’t do that.”

“Be careful, baby. When you play with fire . . .”

“I know.”

“Tell me about Nick.”

"It was better than I thought it would be. It could have been like old times."

"You talked about old times?" She gave him a questioning look.

"In passing. The time goes pretty quickly. He says he had nothing to do with the murder."

"Is there a criminal in the system that ever said 'I'm guilty as sin'?"

"Not too many."

"Do you believe him?"

"I don't know. But when I mentioned Amber, he got very quiet. He says there's something about Amber's relationship with the congressman and the Ice Maiden that needs looking into."

"You're looking into a murder, not a domestic situation. Family squabbles don't seem to be that important right now."

"Ginny, he's scared. He's afraid they might find some reason to keep him."

"And?"

"And all he can talk about is looking into this problem with his sister."

"Nothing else?" She sipped her Scotch and water. A little at a time. There was a time when she could drink him under the table, but she didn't seem interested in doing that at the moment.

"He said Chilli may have been responsible. He said to look into Rapsta Records, but he emphasized the relationship with Amber. I don't know. And I can't talk to him again until day after tomorrow, right?"

"Right. So what are you going to do?"

"Can you handle things here? Follow the news, stay on

top of the story, find out about Charlie White, and see what happens with Chilli?"

She took another sip of the butterscotch-colored liquid. "Sure. Is Jamie going to approve of you heading down to Florida?"

"Jamie will wet his pants if I tell him I've got a lead. I'm not worried about that."

"I'll work up here. We're as close as the phone, so don't worry."

"Maybe there'll be a little bonus at the end of this story."

"As long as it's cash, baby. As long as it's cash."

He took a long swallow and drained the glass. The alcohol slowly worked its way through his veins. It should have relaxed him, but he still felt wound up, like a giant spring that couldn't be compressed anymore.

"I'll feel a lot better if you're up here feeding me information. T-Beau will probably hang in there for Chilli so you may be able to get some help from him."

"I'm a big girl, Mick. I can handle it. But I told you, one week and I'm out of here."

Sever stood up and stretched his stiff knee. His whole body felt tight. When he was home he could always go down to the Bayfront Gym and beat on a punching bag. When he was on the road he never seemed to find the time. He needed to move, needed to make something happen. Part of the tenseness was his restless spirit.

"Let me make a quick reservation. If I can get out this afternoon I could interview these people and be back by tomorrow night."

"Make your call."

"Then let's take a walk. Do you remember, down by the Smithsonian, there's that carousel. . . ."

Her eyes grew wide with excitement. "They have the prettiest ponies. We rode on that twenty times that one afternoon. Let's do it."

Chapter Twenty-seven

Florida?" Jamie sounded winded, drawing short breaths.

"You've got to cut back on the cigarettes, Jamie."

"We've got travel in the budget, Mick. It's just that . . . what happens back here?"

"Ginny's on the payroll. She's on top of things. And besides, it's only a twenty-four-hour hop."

"Man, I wish you had a cell phone."

"Jamie . . ."

"You can't do this by phone?"

"I don't work well on the phone. I want to look at people when I talk to them. You get a better read on the truth that way."

"Sure, Mick. Florida. We'll see you when?"

"Something happens, you'll hear from me right away. If it doesn't I'll be back day after tomorrow. Ginny's working on some angles. She's checking for priors on the chauffeur and watching the Chilli D situation." He listened to the excitable young man on the other end of the line, sucking on a cigarette. "Jamie, I'm going to get a good story out of this. No one else is going this deep. Trust me, you're going to be a hero."

"No doubt. No doubt. Mick, call me. Jesus, just call me once in a while."

"I'm calling you now, aren't I?"

"Have a good flight."

He left a message on T-Beau's hotel answering service telling him he'd be in touch, grabbed a cab in front of the building, and arrived at the Dulles Airport gate thirty minutes before the flight took off.

He closed his eyes as the plane leveled out. He could see her, looking as young as the first time. She'd laughed out loud. Like a scene out of some sappy movie, they'd climbed on the ponies and grabbed the brass ring as the carousel played reedy organ music that repeated itself over and over again. She'd laughed, and so had he. And as trite as it all seemed, even his cynicism couldn't dampen the moment. It was as if the magic had reappeared and for that moment there was no one else. She reached out and took his hand, tucking hers inside his, and they held on to each other for a complete revolution.

"Hey, Nick asked about you. Wondered why we couldn't make it work. Then he made a little remark about the two of you. Something in your past I should have known about?"

She jumped down and was walking back toward the hotel as he caught up with her.

"Hey, was it the horse or me?"

"You'd better get something packed. Your plane leaves in a couple of hours."

"Ginny. What the hell was it?"

"The past should be kept in the past." She kept walking at a brisk pace.

Sever's knee ached but he kept up. "What?"

"It was nothing. A flirtation, nothing more. And you have no room to judge anyone."

"Alright, I did a lot of crazy things."

"So did I. Things you don't even know about."

"Did you have an affair with my best friend?"

"Is that your question? I don't believe it! We're no longer a couple, Mick. Let's keep things in the present, okay?"

He'd been stung. And she was right. There were no more ties, so he had no right to be upset with her.

"How long have we been divorced?" She turned to him, her eyes glistening with tears. "I still hear stories from the road. People love to talk about *your* escapades. I guess they think that since we're not together it's all right to tell me now. Mick did this girl, Mick did that girl, Mick and a porno actress, Mick and the Mötley Crüe party, Mick and some girl trio. People have this need to tell me what they think I missed while we were married. And they have this need to tell me how it is now."

"At the risk of upsetting you even more, I feel I should point out that you weren't exactly the virgin princess."

"No. But a lot of it was me looking for someplace, something, to hold on to. I certainly didn't have you."

"That's a great excuse. Is that a reason to have an affair with Nick Brand?" His heart pounded and he could actually feel the blood coursing through his veins.

"I never admitted to that. Don't you start with me, you cheating son-of-a-bitch!" Sever could see the fire in her eyes.

"What if I've changed?"

"I know you. You still want every girl you see. You still can't settle down and you still have no idea what you want out of life. You're still a little kid, Mick."

"The maturity card. Come on, it's a little late in life to be playing that one." She still pushed his buttons. Damn. "And besides, what brought this on? All I did was mention that Nick talked about you. You've got a wonderful way of turning things around."

"I'm sorry. Things between us can get very confusing. They were then, they are now. We're not a couple anymore. So no matter what I feel for you now, even if I still think about what might be . . ."

He squeezed his eyes shut, trying to clear his head. "What?" He opened them and she was still there, tears now streaming down her cheeks. "You still . . . ?" He couldn't finish the sentence.

"Look." She wiped her eyes with her sleeve. "I said I'd stay and do the job. That's it. No more merry-go-rounds." She picked up the pace and kept on walking. The cool afternoon breeze rustled the late-October leaves and Sever felt the slight chill. No more words were spoken on the way back to the hotel.

Chapter Twenty-eight

He studied the cute first-class flight attendant as she catered to her passengers. She seemed to be familiar with two of them as they shared a joke and a laugh. His day had not been full of laughs. Sever released the back of the seat. Sipping the smooth Chivas Regal, he let his mind work over the events of the day. A funeral, two jailhouse interviews, an insinuation that his former friend had a fling with his ex, and the revelation that Ginny still had feelings for him. Maybe needing that affirmation in itself was a sign of immaturity, but it made him feel a hell of a lot better. The one true friend he had in this world still cared about him. It freed up his mind to work on some other problems.

Somebody killed Bob Shapply. Chilli D appeared to be the only suspect that they had. Chilli D implicated Nick Brand. Was Nick involved? He had motive. Hell, he wanted to go with his gut feeling that his friend, or former friend, was being totally honest with him. Was someone using the

$250,000 loan to Chilli as a weapon? A way to accuse Brand of setting up the murder? He thought about the callous, carefree life they'd led in the early days. Nicky Brand *could* have set it up. Sever hated to admit that, but Nicky could have done it.

And there was Alicia Shapply, T-Beau, and Amber Brand, and the possibility of a whole cast of rappers and managers and record companies that he hadn't even considered yet.

The task of sorting through all the details was daunting, almost overwhelming. He pulled out his laptop and started the job of outlining. The topics, the headings, the subtitles. The devil was in the details. But you had to have all the details first.

Amber Brand was in the book. The only A. Brand listed. Her answering machine was brief. "This is Amber. You know the routine." He hung up and walked to the National Car Rental stand. The little guy who rented him the Chrysler convertible told him he used to be a clown with Ringling Brothers.

"Those were the days, boy. This was circus town."

Sever got directions to Constitution Street, off of Tamiami Trail, a quiet side street with the Siesta Key Marina on the corner, then stucco house after stucco house, each with its own obligatory palm and brightly colored croton tree. The rough Florida grass was clipped short and a lack of rain gave the lawns a brownish green hue with patches of bare earth and sand peeking through.

He parked on the street, three houses away, and walked to the faded yellow house. A gray striped cat peered between two plastic garbage cans, hissing at him as he approached the porch. Sever punched the doorbell and waited.

The door swung open with a loud creak, and a skinny man in a stained undershirt and boxer shorts stood there, looking accusingly at him. The thin man brushed his long greasy hair from his face and stared intently at Sever.

"You from welfare?"

"No. I came to see Amber."

"You from child support? Some agency, right?"

Sever looked beyond the man, into the dimly lit room beyond. He could see that the television was on, a Jerry Springer show with every other word beeped out. Clothes were strewn on a sofa and chair and the whole place seemed to have a disheveled appearance.

"Look, I'm a friend. A friend of her brother." It was strange even saying it. He had no friends. And Nick was not a friend anymore.

"You bringin' any money?"

"I'm not sure who you expected."

"If you don't have any money, buddy, then I got no reason to talk to you." He stepped back and pushed the door. Sever stuck out his foot and held it from closing.

The unkempt man spun around, fire in his eyes. "Hey, asshole. I think I told you to leave."

Sever shoved the door open with his foot and walked into the living room. "I came to see Amber. Not to give you any money, or to start a fight. I need to talk to her, and I would appreciate it if you'd tell me where she is."

The shrill scream from the top of the stairs startled him. He glanced up, expecting to see a body hurtling down the worn carpeted steps.

The man looked up and shouted. "Shut the fuck up!"

Sever watched him look at the ceiling as if his vision could penetrate the yellowed tile.

"Who's up there?"

"It's the kid. The kid's watching the baby and when the baby cries, the kid screams, and . . . fuck it. Get the fuck out if you're not from an agency."

Sever turned and started up the steps. He smelled the sour odor of the man close behind and felt the hand close on his shoulder.

"Do you have a problem with me going up?"

The man hesitated. "Nah! Fuck it. I really don't care." He turned and walked back down the stairs.

Sever continued up the short flight.

"Who are you?" The little girl's face was flush, her brown hair plastered to the shape of her face from the stifling humidity and heat.

"Are you Margarite?"

"Are you from welfare?"

"No, I'm a friend of your mother. Is she home?"

"No. Josh is watching us." She rolled her eyes and shrugged her shoulders.

Sever looked down the stairs but saw no sign of Josh.

"My mother is working. She cleans office buildings at night."

"And the baby is . . . ?"

"Oh. The baby is Josh's little girl. Her mommy is in jail so she lives here." Once again she rolled her eyes. The young girl seemed to understand the situation better than the adult downstairs.

"I'm Mick. I used to be . . ." He stumbled. It was tough

bringing the right words to the situation, even if he was talking to a twelve-year-old. "I used to be best friends with your uncle Nick."

"Oh."

"I'm in town for just tonight. Could you tell me where your mother might be?"

"Josh knows. He's got a phone number for every office she cleans. Mom doesn't trust him, so she leaves the numbers so he can call if he has a problem."

"Well, is the baby all right?"

"The baby is fine. I just don't like her crying all the time. It makes me . . ."

"Want to scream?"

Margarite broke into a grin. "How did you do that?"

"I don't know. I just knew that's what you were going to say."

She nodded. "I've got to change her diaper. Josh won't touch her."

"Thanks for the information. I hope I meet you again."

"I'll tell Mom you stopped by." She opened the hall closet, pulled out a disposable diaper, and turned back toward one of the bedrooms. Sever saw the poise and maturity of an adult. Thank goodness there was one in the house.

He walked down the stairs and saw the tough guy sitting in front of the TV. Springer had been replaced with *The Simpsons*.

"Where are the phone numbers for Amber's offices?"

Without looking up, Josh motioned to a vinyl-topped table. Next to the phone was a pad. Sever tore off a sheet of paper and wrote the numbers from the front of the tablet onto the paper. He tried the first number and was greeted with an answering machine. The second number was the same. The third time a man picked up the phone.

"Is Amber there? The lady who cleans the office?"

Silence. Then a female voice. "Hello? Josh? Is there a problem."

"Amber? This is Mick Sever."

"Jesus Christ. This is a joke. Who is this?"

"Seriously."

"You . . . Mick, I . . ."

"Amber, I need to talk to you. Can we get together maybe tonight?"

"I . . ." She was virtually speechless.

"Amber. I need to see you."

Finally she seemed to get herself together. "Do you know that twenty years ago I would have done just about anything to hear that?"

"Is there somewhere we could meet?"

"Yes! Yes! There's a Denny's at One North Tamiami Trail. I can be there at about eleven-thirty. This is really you?"

"It's really me."

"Mick. Mick Sever."

He smiled. The little sister. It sounded as if she'd had a crush on him for a long time.

Chapter Twenty-nine

Four cars sat in the parking lot, two from out of state. A Mercedes and a rusted-out station wagon with Sarasota plates were his choices. He bet on the station wagon.

She sat at the counter, a steaming cup of coffee in front of her, puffing on a long thin cigarette. Amber glanced at him as he walked in, then turned nervously back to her coffee and took a sip. Looking up again, her eyes grew wide.

"It is you."

"Why not?"

"Because . . . because. Why would you come to see me? It's about Dad, isn't it? And Nick." He hadn't seen her since she was a kid. The face was rounder, almost no makeup, and her hair was tied back. She appeared to be slightly overweight, but he could still see the basic features he remembered. The nose that turned up slightly. The piercing brown eyes, and the high cheekbones. The same features he'd seen a short time ago in her twelve-year-old daughter.

"Sure. Your mother and Nick are both worried about you, and since I'm doing a piece on your father's—"

"Bullshit! The day my mother worries about me hell will freeze over."

Sever couldn't help but smile. Why was he trying to fool the Ice Maiden's daughter?

"You think that's funny?" She squinted at him, fire shooting from her eyes.

"No. I've known your mother for a long time. There's nothing remotely funny about her. But she did express concern. She's somehow afraid that you're going to try to drag your father's reputation through the mud because of his will."

Amber took a lungful of smoke and let it drift out in a slow steady stream. "That's what she told you? God's honest truth?"

"That's what she told me."

"Margarite called and said you stopped by the house."

"She's a sharp kid. Very mature for her age."

Amber seemed mellow. The outburst was behind her. "She's had to grow up quickly. You saw the place. You see my car when you drove in?"

"The Mercedes?"

She giggled. "Yeah. That's the one. Mick, I don't have much. And if something was offered from my mother or father I'd probably turn it down. I don't want anything from them. I don't even want people to know that I'm related."

"Things were that bad at home? Your father seems to have died a wealthy man. Your mother obviously wants for very little. What could be so bad that you'd turn down a better lifestyle?"

She said nothing, puffing on the cigarette, dangerously

close to the filter. Stubbing it out in her ashtray, she drained the rest of her coffee and stood up.

"I've got to go."

"Wait a minute. About three hours ago you were excited I was here. What happened?"

"I didn't expect the third degree."

Sever put his hand on her arm. "Maybe we need to start over again. I flew a long way to see you, and I don't want to see this end before it begins."

"What do you want to know?"

"I don't want this to come off like the third degree. However, I do have some questions. Can we sit in a booth? This counter is very impersonal."

They moved to a vinyl booth and the waitress brought him a Coke.

"Josh?"

"Third degree?"

"Okay, you tell me where to start."

She reached up and patted down her hair, an imagined strand now back in place.

"I'm sorry. You've got questions, ask them. I'm just not in a place where I want to talk about the relationship with my parents."

"Then talk about Josh and Margarite."

"Josh is a boyfriend. He's"—she hesitated—"he's my CBF."

"Don't know that one."

"Convenience boyfriend."

"What's convenient?" Sever folded his hands in front of him. She was starting to open up and he didn't want to push too hard.

"He's got a job. Not a great job. He's a short-order cook during the day and watches Margarite at night. That's convenient."

"I think Margarite is under the impression that she watches him."

Amber rolled her eyes. "She does. But it all works out. And due to our hours, we don't have to see each other very often. And that's convenient, too." She laughed out loud. "It's a strange life, Mick. Not the life I imagined, but it works. And at the center is Margarite. Sweet, lovable Margarite."

"Amber, I don't want to pry, but it's my job. Let me ask you this. If Margarite is the center of your universe, then why would you deprive her of family money?"

She took a deep breath, pulled a Virginia Slim from her purse, and lit it with a cheap plastic lighter. Sever smelled the first hint of smoke, wishing he had a cigarette, too.

"Mick, there's a lot of history. You were tight with Nick, so you knew things that happened. My father was abusive, abusive as hell, and my mother withdrew and refused to deal with it. My father was a crook! Hell, who knows better than you? But there were other things. Things I can't talk about. He claims he was saved by my uncle, the Reverend Joseph Evans. But it's bullshit. Mick, I just can't go there right now. Can you please accept that?"

"Okay. Let me ask you this." He placed his hand on top of hers. He wanted to be reassuring, but he needed some answers. "Do you have any idea who killed your father?"

She left her hand on the table. "No. I've thought about it and I really don't know. I think there were a lot of people who didn't like him, and I know there were a lot of people that he stepped on over the years. I know he was going after a very strong group of people in the record business, and there's a violent element there. Notorious BIG, Tupac, Puffy—take your pick. And a lot of people had it out for my dad. I think that group would do anything to protect themselves."

"Nick sends his greetings."

"Is he still in jail?"

"Yeah. They think he set it up."

"Something you don't know. Nick fought Dad long and hard about what happened to you. They had a parting of the ways and I don't think he ever talked to Dad after that. He always believed that he'd destroyed the friendship between the two of you."

Sever gazed out the window, watching the cars pass by on the Trail. Even though it was midnight there was a steady stream of traffic.

"You know, I wanted to believe that he didn't want to be involved, but . . ."

"He didn't. You were his inspiration. He looked up to you, a self-made guy. Nick always had Dad to point the way, but you were what he aspired to."

"He's successful. Making big deals with the stars, he seems to have done all right."

"Following in Dad's footsteps. That's the way he sees it."

"Amber, I've got some serious questions and we've both had a long day. Any chance we could pick this up tomorrow? I could stop by for a cup of coffee, while Josh—"

"Flips burgers? I'd enjoy that. It'll give me time to think. I don't have the answers you want, but I may be able to tell you where they are."

"Could Nick have killed your father?"

She stared through him. "There were times. There were

times I could have." She stood up and headed toward the door.

They walked to their cars, and she slid into the station wagon and drove away, one rear taillight winking at him as she made her exit. Sever stretched his leg, the familiar twinge in the knee letting him know he'd been sitting much too long. He took a long slow breath, smelling the damp, musty ocean breeze. He could be down in the Keys right now, sipping a margarita and saying "to hell with the rest of the world." He climbed into the rental car and drove off searching for a motel down the road. Amber said she knew where to look, and that sounded promising. Maybe the trip to Sarasota would pan out. Jamie would be so happy.

Chapter Thirty

He woke up a desk clerk at a small place on Siesta Key. The chain hotels were all around, but staying down by the water in this little bedroom/kitchenette was, in a small way, like being in Key West. He walked the wide white sand beach lit by the platinum moon and passed the occasional lovers holding hands, the old men who were wondering when the tide would stop rolling in, and the people like himself who seemed somewhat lost but were hoping to find themselves in the ancient ocean. The crash of the waves was music, like cymbals in a symphony. The late-night call of the gulls were woodwinds and flutes playing a melody with the percussion. He walked a mile, maybe two, then wearily hobbled back to his small unit, his leg aching with pain. A good pain. The ocean rejuvenated his soul.

The knee was a constant reminder of his drug days, and nights. He'd taken a header off of a stage, and was damned lucky to be alive. He couldn't forget the night, no matter how hard he tried. The pain was always there. For some unfathomable reason Sever was still among the living.

He woke in the very early morning. Gritting his teeth, he walked a block to a 7-Eleven store. A cup of black coffee, a newspaper, and a bottle of Bayer. He needed something to get him through the morning.

At 10 A.M. he headed out and parked on the street in front of Amber's house about 10:15. She yelled at the door, "Come in." Amber was sitting at the kitchen table, looking the same as she had the night before. The coffee was steaming and she was drawing on a Virginia Slim, blowing smoke rings at the ceiling.

"Is this a good time?

"It's a great time. Margarite is in school, Josh is at work, and the baby is asleep. For how long I can't be certain, but for the moment it's a great time." She shoved the sleeves of her gray sweatshirt up over her elbows. The snug jeans did little to hide her ample thighs and hips. "Coffee?"

"Sure."

She motioned to the pot on the stove. Sever helped himself. "Had time to think?"

"You want information on my father's murder. I don't have that information."

"You told me you might know where that information is."

"I can't talk to you about that. There are some personal issues I have that I just can't share with you. I barely know you. I'm not even sure I could talk to Nick."

"Tell me about your daughter."

"She's the love of my life. She makes me want to do better every day, every minute."

"Her name?"

"After a friend. Do you remember?"

"Yeah. She was killed, right?"

"Uh-huh." She had a distant look in her eyes.

"Barbados?"

"Dad took us on vacation. He had an interest in a recording studio over there. Mick Jagger had a house there, and some other rock stars, and Dad thought it would be a good place to invest. There were a couple of major-league studios. So Dad bought an interest in one, with other people's money. He was good at that. And then he flew a couple of recording acts over there to use the facility. It was all some kind of scheme so he could launder a whole bunch of money."

"You knew all of this at the age of twelve?"

"No. I learned about it afterwards. I've done a lot of research on that trip, Mick. My best friend lost her life over there."

"Your dad owned part of a recording studio and a couple of rock acts?"

"Uh-huh."

"And the money he was illegally taking from his clients in the States . . ."

"He was spending in Barbados. It was a good way to hide it."

That's where the money went. Ginny would be surprised to learn that their one and a half million had helped launch bands in Barbados. Sever sipped at the coffee.

"So you, your mom and dad, Margarite, and a couple of rock bands were in Barbados?"

"What I remember is that we stayed on the south end of the island. There was a hotel with some very fancy suites and we lay on the beach every day and swam in the pool and hired a full-time guy, Phillip, who watched us, fed us, drove us, whatever we needed. Phillip Teese. He was a sweet guy. I know we took advantage of him every chance we got. We'd sneak out and go down to the topless section of the beach, check out the naked bodies, or we'd head up to this little bar and sweet-talk the owner into letting us split a beer. Margarite and I thought we'd hit the jackpot."

"Phillip doesn't sound like he was very attentive."

"He thought we both were harmless."

"What happened? Did this Teese drop his guard? Did Margarite get killed on his watch?"

"You know, I'd rather not talk about this."

He was in *her* house, drinking *her* coffee. He pressed his advantage. "Somebody killed her. Were you with her?"

"It was a long time ago. I don't know what happened."

"You said you've been looking into it."

"Mick, I don't know what happened. I've asked a million questions, I've spent thousands of dollars. Since I was fifteen or sixteen I've been obsessed with it. I even saved enough money and flew back there two years ago. I've talked to the musicians who were there. I've talked to the people who were involved in the recording studio. The older I get, the more I want to know why!" She was shaking, and her hands were clasped tight. Tears ran down her face and he knew he'd gone too far. He couldn't stop.

"Amber, what did you learn?"

"Nothing. I've done nothing but stirred up memories and sadness." She wiped the tears with a napkin and lit another cigarette. Her eyes were streaked with red and she rattled the coffee cup against the table as she picked it up to take a sip. "Damn. It's cold."

"What happened to the studio?"

"It's still there."

"And?"

"My father's partner still runs it. And he won't talk to me. He and my dad are very, *were* very close."

"And you think he had something to do with her death?"

"I don't know. His name is Bobby Jergan. He was and is a snake."

"A snake?"

"He's slimy. He won't look you in the eye. The rumor I heard was he was not only helping spend my father's laundered money, but he was dealing drugs, too."

"But there's no connection to this Bobby Jergan and your father's death?"

"I don't know. Yes! Maybe. I think whoever killed Margarite may be involved in my father's death."

"What's the connection? Can you explain that?"

"I can't!" She exploded. "Damn it, Mick. I believe it, but I can't tell you why."

"All right." His voice was calm. "What happened that night?"

"We were all partying on the beach. Some local band was playing and there were island celebrities like Eddie Grant—remember him? He did 'Electric Avenue,' and I remember all the adults drinking and laughing; it was one of the few times I can remember my mother getting loose, you know? She sang and danced. Really. She was actually human. And Bobby Jergan, Dad, Mom, the band, and Margarite, we were all just enjoying the moment. Margarite and I were playing on the beach, running into the tide, trying to catch it as it slipped away. One minute she was there, the next she had disappeared.

We found her the next morning." The baby let out a single yelp, then started sobbing. "I knew it was too good to be true."

"What could this possibly have to do with your father's death?"

"I don't know that it does, Mick. I'm an emotional mess when it comes to this story. Ask Bobby Jergan. He was there, and I think he knows more than he's telling."

"Is it worth a trip over there?"

"I told you, whoever killed Margarite may be involved in my father's death. What else do you want me to say?" She pushed the chair back and started up the stairs. The volume of wailing increased.

"It was good to see you again."

She paused and looked back at him. "Was it? Did you get what you came for?" She turned and walked up the rest of the stairs. He let himself out and drove to the airport.

There was no point in talking to anyone else. He was convinced she hadn't given him everything she knew. She was going to make him work for that, but he had enough information to be dangerous.

Chapter Thirty-one

Sever sat in the lounge and sipped an ice-cold Corona. He let the amber fluid lie on his tongue then slide down his throat, savoring the squeezed lime that provided that unique tart, tangy taste. Flipping through the tablet, he reviewed the notes. They were fresh in his mind. Someday he'd like to go back and apologize for his attitude. Like a bulldozer, he just kept digging. Amber had some serious issues and maybe it wasn't the best idea in the world to push her like he had, but everyone had issues. You just learned to deal with them. Sever left the beer and his notes on the table and walked a few steps to the pay phone. He called Ginny at the hotel.

"Hi. Are we talking again?"

"Yes. It was silly. I'm sorry, Mick. We've got to quit living in the past."

"Yeah, we do."

"Speaking of the past, I was thinking about us last night, and something my mom said. And for some reason I started laughing and I couldn't stop. It wasn't that funny, but I can just picture her."

"What was it?"

"Remember that Billy Joel song? About Virginia . . . 'Only the Good Die Young.' That's it. Mom was talking about you, and she quoted the line, 'the only thing he'll give you is a reputation.' I just thought it was extremely funny. My mom, quoting Billy Joel, and that quote."

"And I did."

"And you did. Hey, you, what did you find in Florida?"

"Let's start with you. What have you found?"

"Charlie White. He appears to be clean. It wasn't too tough to track him because the limo company did a preliminary background check when they hired him. The man gambled a little, played the horses, and his wife put a private detective on his case one time to see if he was having an affair."

"Was he?"

"Yeah."

"Nothing else?"

"No, but do you remember what T-Beau suggested? The chauffeur sets up the shooting or shoots Robert Shapply, then someone shoots *him* to keep him quiet. Charlie White knew when the congressman was coming home. And he knew when he'd be driving you and Alicia Shapply around town. No one else had those two pieces of information."

"No one else sees it like that?"

"They think they have their killer. They produced the gun that Chilli supposedly used to shoot Shapply."

"So, that looks more and more like it's a closed deal."

"Haven't gotten too far with Nick. They're charging him with being an accessory, and I don't know what proof they have."

"They seemed pretty certain they had enough to make it stick."

"Tell me about Amber."

"You're going to think I'm crazy, Ginny. She believes her father's death has something to do with a business deal and murder in Barbados twenty years ago."

"You want to hear something crazy? I don't know if you've been near a television in the last twenty-four hours, but Amber's uncle has been on almost every network and cable news show in the country saying that the music industry is behind the death of his brother-in-law. He's determined to have those hearings and pick up where Shapply left off."

Sever watched her cautiously. "Did you hear what I said? A murder in Barbados?"

Ginny was silent. "Ginny?"

"I know, Mick. Just a day or two is all you need to track down the sources. It's your gut reaction, but I can hold down the fort while you just check it out to see if there's anything to it and—"

"Hey. Why do I bother to exist since you can be the two of us at the same time."

"God! I know you. You tell me how much you hate this drive to explore every last detail, and then you throw yourself at the next one. Do you really want to go to Barbados?"

"I'm sitting at an airport. You're following up the leads that we've got in Washington. I can get to Barbados, interview two or three people, visit this recording studio that Shapply had an interest in, and be back in time to relieve you so you can go back to work on whatever other project you're dealing with."

"Mick, it's your story. I'll be here. Tomorrow I thought I'd have a sit-down with Nick. There are some things I want to ask him, and maybe he'll tell me some things that he wouldn't tell you."

Sever held his tongue. No more questions about Nick and Ginny. "I'm going. Do me a favor."

"Hey, as if I'm not already?"

"I'm sorry, Gin. I take you for granted. But please, do me one more favor. Call Beau. Tell him I'm going to try to book a flight out today. He did some recording in Barbados about twenty years ago. It would be great if he could fly in and meet me. I could cover more territory with two of us and he probably knows the island."

"And what about Chilli D?"

"I don't think he's going anywhere. Hell, if we can find a motive in Barbados, maybe we can figure out what happened."

"And what about Jamie?"

"Oh yeah. The guy who's picking up the tab for all this. Tell him I'm following some good leads and I'll be in touch."

"I'm sure he'll be thrilled."

"Ginny, I owe you."

"You'll never be able to pay back all the IOUs I've got." They were both quiet for a moment. "Oh, Mick. Did you piss off a guy with greasy black hair and a complexion like he washes with a Brillo pad?"

"What?"

"This very obnoxious guy stopped me outside the hotel this morning. Actually grabbed my arm. He asked me if I was

Ginny Sever. When I told him yes, he said 'Tell your boyfriend I've got a surprise for him when he gets home.' That was it, and he walked away."

"Shit. It's one of the guys we had the run-in with."

"The one you punched out?"

"Yeah. If you see him again, call the cops. You can't take a chance. . . ."

"I'm a big girl. I can take care of myself. I've got to go."

"Ginny, seriously. Maybe you should just forget about—"

"'Bye, Mick. Behave yourself!" She was gone.

He returned to his seat, but the beer was warm and the lime was sour. He left it on the table and headed for the ticket counter.

Chapter Thirty-two

Writers described the ocean as blue. From the plane the waters of the Caribbean were pale green, the intensity of color changing as the reefs and sand bars appeared and disappeared. From thirty thousand feet he could still see boats, ships, tankers carrying oil, and ocean liners carrying well-to-do passengers covered with oil who had nothing to do but eat, drink, and bask on the deck in the golden sunlight. It was what he longed for, the perfect getaway, and at the same time he knew it would end up boring him to death.

Sever's American Express card was hot to the touch. A last-minute first-class trip to Barbados was not cheap, and he knew Jamie would have a fit when he got the final bill. If there wasn't a story here, Sever had decided to pick up the tab himself. It remained to be seen if T-Beau would make the flight over. And it remained to be seen if the *New York Hustle* would pick up the tab for Beau just for the thrill of having the Love Doctor's name on a story. He figured they probably would.

With barely any luggage and nothing to declare he cleared customs easily. Grabbing a taxi he had the driver drop him off at the Bougainvillea, a suite hotel and resort on the southern end of the island that was frequented by British tourists. The room was typical for a Caribbean resort, with a huge ceiling fan centered directly over the king-size bed, a living-room area with tropical cane chairs and a sofa, a fully equipped kitchen, and a patio overlooking the pool and beach. He placed a call to Washington and Ginny answered on the first ring.

"Mick, I've got some information. First of all, T-Beau is on his way. He said he didn't trust you to be on your own over there, and he could help grease the skids, whatever that means. Second, the Ice Maiden called."

"Alicia Shapply called you?"

"Yeah. She was trying to find you. I told her you were on your way over to—"

"Probably not a good idea."

"You're right."

"I am?"

"She got very upset. She said that what happened in Barbados had nothing to do with what happened in Washington and you should keep your nose out of her personal business."

"She said that?"

"I'm not making this up. She was right to the point. Said, 'tell him to drop his little investigation.' She said she was sorry she'd ever mentioned Amber's situation and she hinted that she could make things very unpleasant for you if you didn't just leave it alone."

"Hell, she's the one who started the ball rolling."

"I got the distinct impression she was very sorry that she did."

Sever moved to the balcony and watched a young lady in a thong bikini down by the pool. She strutted in front of two portly men in tight-fitting Speedos. Sever wouldn't be caught in one of those European bathing suits. These guys were obscene. The woman, however, was gorgeous. He looked away and concentrated on the problem at hand.

"What are you looking for over there?"

"I don't know. I've got some names and some places. If they seem to fit into the puzzle, then I'll try to put it together. Amber and Nick both seemed to think something over here is responsible for what happened in Washington."

"Well, Mrs. Shapply is not happy that you're over there. And she made a very direct threat. Watch yourself!"

"It makes no sense. When is T-Beau arriving?"

"He should be there in a couple of hours." Ginny gave him the flight number and time. "Mick, don't push your luck. This is just a story. You're not a cop, you're not a lawyer."

"I know. But something happened over here. And it goes further than just finding out who killed Bob Shapply."

"How much further?"

"This sounds crazy, but I get the impression that if I find the right answers it may help me come to terms with the Nick Brand situation."

"Mick, it's a story. You've had a million of them and you'll have a million more. I think you're putting way too much pressure on yourself."

"Maybe it's about time I did. Any sign of the greasy-haired guy?"

"I haven't seen him."

"Ginny, seriously. This story isn't worth you getting hurt."

"This from a guy who's been shot at and attacked on the street?"

"Be careful, babe, I care about you."

He watched the white-capped waves crashing onto the beach, laughing children scampering away from them then spinning around and chasing the water back out as it receded into the ocean. Over and over again, like a never-ending story. Maybe it was just a story, like all the stories before, repeating themselves over and over again.

"Mick, I care about you, too."

"I'll call you soon." Sever hung up the phone and eased into a lounge chair on the deck. He closed his eyes and let the warm sunshine soak into his tired body.

Chapter Thirty-three

Can't have you over here by yourself, muckin' up everything. There's a certain balance here in Barbados, you know what I'm sayin'? You just gonna fuck it up without the Love Doctor to guide you through." T-Beau laughed from his belly and pushed his one suitcase into the back of the van. The driver nodded and opened the door for him, then eased out of the airport and started the twenty-five-minute drive to the hotel.

"Dave said the drive is usually half the time but they've got the streets totally ripped up for a new sewer project."

"Dave?"

"T-Beau, meet Dave."

The driver turned around and gave them a toothy grin. "Good to meet you. I've had some remarkable times listening to your music."

"Hey, Dave. I've had some remarkable times making my music." T-Beau turned to Sever. "Shit, man, these streets are always ripped up for some reason. Last time I was here and the time before they was all torn up. I think they're workin' on island time. Take two or three years to do what it takes a month to do in the States."

The van ran down the left side of the road, Dave veering to miss potholes and uneven sections of pavement. Occasionally a car would approach in the right lane and Sever would stifle the urge to yell. Even if you weren't driving, it took a while to get used to vehicles on the reverse side of the road.

"Sugarcane." T-Beau looked wistfully out the window at the green-leaved plants growing in the fields. "'Member the song? 'Sugar Cane'?"

"Sure. It did very well for you."

"Wrote it over here. There was this little island girl, she'd mix me rum drinks and squeeze some raw cane into 'em. Sweet stuff. She was like that raw cane. Squeeze her and the sweetness just come runnin' out. I wrote that song about her and that raw cane."

"What made you decide to come over?"

"Like I told you, can't have you over here muckin' things up. I know people. Maybe I can help get to the bottom of whatever it is you're lookin' for."

"I don't know for sure what it is."

"Amber seems to think there's somethin' here that could shed some light on her daddy's murder? I want to get Chill off. Maybe we can scratch each other's back."

"From what Ginny tells me it doesn't look good for Chilli."

"It doesn't. It sure doesn't look good, Mick. I hope we stumble on somethin' over here."

The sugarcane fields and cotton fields gave way to houses,

fancy homes higher in the hills and clapboard wood and small stucco homes by the side of the road.

"Chattel houses." Dave pointed to the row of wooden houses, faded pastel colors and wooden runners on the sides. "Used to move them from plantation to plantation. The men who worked the fields just moved the whole house."

The partially paved road veered sharply, and pedestrian traffic picked up as women walked the side of the pavement heading for a shop or just out for a stroll. Dave would occasionally slow down and lean out the window talking to some of them in his own language.

Sever leaned over to T-Beau. "Patois?"

"Over here it's called Bajan. Their own private language. Kind of like Brooklyn English, if you know what I mean."

They came in the back way, past the Ship's Horn restaurant and the Dover cricket field.

"Cricket?" Sever nodded at the sign. "Now there's a sport I know nothing about."

Dave honked and waved at an old lady who wobbled unsteadily as she walked, either a physical ailment or too much to drink too early in the day. She smiled and waved back. "Cricket. It's the national sport," Dave said.

T-Beau leaned up from the backseat. "Be honest with me, Dave. Do you understand the game? Man, I watched cricket over here, and I'm tellin' you the truth, I never understood what it was I was lookin' at. You get points for hittin', points for missin', and points for I don't know what all!"

Dave laughed. "It's an acquired sport, my friend. I visit my cousin in New York and we go see your New York Mets. He's explained the rules to me many times and I have yet to understand the infield fly rule, or what happens if the catcher drops the ball on the first or second strike or how it's played if he drops it on the third strike, and—"

"I'm hip! If you don't grow up with the sport, it takes some serious learning."

Dave dropped them off at the open-air lobby, the smell of jasmine and coconut oil wafting through the palm trees.

"Smells like home, Mick!" T-Beau filled his sizable chest with the sweet fragrance and put his head back. "Shit, baby, it is sweet to be back!" A small boy in a bright yellow swimsuit and carrying a bucket in his hand looked up at the noise and shrieked.

They sat at a table by the bar, under the canopy, sipping cold Banks beer from the bottle and watching the whitecap waves hurling themselves at the shore. The slightly bitter brown beverage slid down their throats and cut through the sweet taste of the broiled mahimahi they'd finished moments ago.

"Good food." T-Beau stretched out his legs.

The dark-skinned waitress in the tailored, uniformed jacket put fresh beers on the table. She gave them both a wide smile, lingering beside T-Beau. "I don't often ask for autographs, management frowns on it, but . . ."

She handed him a napkin and a pen. "Sting was here a couple of weeks ago but he was surrounded by all these people and his wife and—"

"What's your name?"

"Lucinda."

"Pretty. Should have written a song named 'Lucinda.' "

She smiled softly, falling under the charm.

"If you're free later and you got a nice friend, maybe we can sit under the stars and have a few drinks."

"Really?"

"If we run into each other, it will be a night to remember."

She walked off, giving them a show with her hips swaying. "Keep the options open, Mick." T-Beau watched her retreat. "Never know what's gonna present itself."

"Dave's picking us up in half an hour. We'll head up to the recording studio, about thirty-five minutes from here."

"Haven't been there in years. You say Bobby Jergan is still there?"

"I called Bajan Sound. I didn't tell them who I was, but they said he'd be in this afternoon. I don't want him to be prepared."

"Surprise him. He'll sure as hell be surprised to see me. Maybe not too happy."

"You had a run-in with this guy?"

"Did some backup stuff for the man. Sang on a couple albums for him and the son-of-a-bitch never paid me. Only a couple thousand dollars, but back then I could have used it, you know what I'm sayin'?"

"This guy had the nerve not to pay you?"

"I was younger. I figured it was a lesson in the business."

"So you're looking forward to seeing this guy? Should be a real homecoming."

They were quiet, listening to the Caribbean symphony—seagulls, the crash of the waves, and island music playing through the speakers by the pool.

"Place got it's own rhythm, Mick. Gotta let it get inside you. If there's secrets here, get close to the rhythm. You'll find 'em."

Sever shook his head. "Voodoo, Beau. Let's get into the real world. Alicia Shapply doesn't want me over here looking into this thing. She was adamant with Ginny."

"Let the old bones rest? Hell, she was the reason you went down to see Amber. She opened up this can of worms."

"She simply wanted me to talk to Nick. *I* decided to take it to the next level."

"And now this level." T-Beau drained the rest of his beer and eased out of the chair. "I'm gonna freshen up a little. Wanta look my best for Bobby Jergan." He ambled back toward the hotel, drawing inquisitive looks from the poolside tourists.

Chapter Thirty-four

That's the biggest rum factory on the island." Dave pointed in the distance, through the cane fields. "Lots of jobs, lots of rum."

The van rumbled over the rough-paved narrow roads. "What you gonna ask Mr. Jergan?" T-Beau had changed to an expansive polo shirt, pressed linen slacks, and brown sandals. He turned his head and looked out the rear window.

"I don't know. I seriously don't know. I need to find out what happened on the beach that night. And I'm sure he's not going to just volunteer the information."

Few cars passed them, and the swaying of the van and the meandering road lulled them into silence. Occasionally a chuckhole shook the vehicle, rattling the van with the force of a minor collision.

"You go through a lot of shocks, Dave?" T-Beau turned and glanced out the rear window again.

"I would be broke if I bought them when I needed them.

We turn off the road up here. It's back a dirt road, about two miles."

"Dave?" T-Beau leaned up to the driver's seat. "Small wood-panel truck behind us been goin' this way ever since we left the hotel. What else is up this road?"

"Plantation houses. This road connects with lots of other roads. Probably locals."

"Slow it down before you head back to the studio. Just let 'em pass."

Sever glanced at him, then turned and saw the truck running a safe distance behind them. Dave slowed it down to a crawl.

The truck slowly closed the gap, then passed on the right.

"Guess they was just out for a drive."

The brake lights flashed and the truck stopped. The doors opened and two young men in T-shirts stepped out.

"Can you step on it?" T-Beau had fire in his eyes. "Get around 'em and get down the road?"

Sever saw it first. The glint of the shotgun barrel held closely to the young man's leg. The man slowly swung it up until it was pointed directly at the window of the van. Dave jammed on the brake and stopped.

"Shit, shoulda run it."

They sat still in the van, the two men in the middle of the road. A Bajan standoff.

Sever glanced at T-Beau. "Somebody's got to make the first move."

"Man holdin' the gun be the one in my book."

Dave held tightly to the steering wheel. "Either one of you gentlemen know a reason why somebody is aimin' a gun at us?"

T-Beau and Sever were silent.

The boy with the gun approached the van. "Get out! All of you."

They opened the doors and he motioned them to line up by the side of the road.

The second man approached them, with what looked like a Banks beer bottle held tightly in his hand. He grabbed Dave by the arm and led him back to the idling van. "Got anything personal in there?"

Dave shook his head. "Just my license and a picture of my family."

"Get 'em!"

Dave climbed in and pulled the license and picture from the visor.

"Stand back." The young man looked back at his partner, holding the shotgun waist level. He glared at them, daring anyone to make the first move. The bottle-wielding man reached into his pocket and pulled out a pack of matches. It was then that Sever noticed the rag stuffed into the bottle's opening.

"Got to be careful who you haul around here on the island, mon. You pick up these foreigners and we have to sanitize your taxi." He smiled at Dave, lit the rag, and underhanded the bottle into the open van door. Nodding to his partner, they took off on a run to the truck.

"Christ, let's get out of here!" Sever grabbed Dave by the elbow as the driver hesitated.

"That's my van. I need my van."

"Run!" Sever yanked his arm and he followed reluctantly. T-Beau was three steps ahead as they ran into the field.

"Down! Down!" Sever shouted, as he threw himself into the sugarcane.

He could feel the heat as he looked over his shoulder. The van was engulfed in flames, black smoke pouring from the windows.

"Mick, you alright?" T-Beau called from nearby.

"Stay down, man! That thing is gonna—"

The explosion was deafening, a thundering blast as a huge orange fireball erupted twenty feet into the air, sending flying pieces of metal and glass hurtling in all directions. Sever felt a piece of hot sharp steel crash down on his shoulder. The pain was almost unbearable. He closed his eyes and could hear the whoosh of air as it was consumed by the fire. He tried to catch a breath but the acrid smoke choked him. Putting his hand over his mouth, he drew a short breath.

"Beau? Are you alright?" He shouted above the roar of the fire.

No sound.

"Dave?"

Coughing. "I'm here. You okay?"

A second explosion, not as loud as the first, thundered down the road. Sever felt hot ash pepper his legs and back. He shook his body and tried to sit up. The stinging pain in his shoulder felt like the attack of one hundred bees. Struggling into a sitting position he surveyed the surroundings.

Black smoke poured from the burned-out frame. The surrounding road and acreage looked like a battlefield, shrapnel scattered everywhere.

Dave was standing, staring at what was left of his former livelihood. His face was scratched from the sugarcane, but other than that he looked in one piece.

"Do you see Beau?"

"No." Dave glanced at him. "Mon! You got a cut on your shoulder. We need to get you to a doctor."

Sever reached up and touched the shoulder gingerly. There was blood, and it ached but it didn't seem to be too bad. He moved the arm. He still had mobility.

"Beau?" He screamed.

"I'm here." The big man was raising up, about twenty yards away.

"So we're all alive?"

"Seem to be."

Dave hung his head. "We got to get back, mon."

"Could have hitched a ride with those two boys, but they seem to have taken off without us." T-Beau pulled a large yellow handkerchief from his pants pocket and approached Sever. He wrapped the rag around the exposed cut, soaking up the blood. "I always knew I'd find a good use for one of these things." He smiled at Mick as the three of them walked to the road.

Chapter Thirty-five

I'm sorry for the situation you find yourself in." The policeman kept a respectful look of concern on his face. "There are trucks that meet that description all over our island. Of course we'll make an effort to find these two young men, but for now, gentlemen, I would suggest you exercise caution when you travel our island."

"We're in Christ Church?"

"Certainly, Mr. Sever. The Bridgetown Division."

"There was an unsolved murder here twenty years ago. A young girl named Margarite Haller. She would have been about twelve years old. Is there anyone around who would remember the case? Or are there records we could see?"

The policeman nodded. "This is a small island. There are not that many murders. Maybe ten a year. I know we have the records of that case, and possibly I can find someone who worked on it personally. Can I have the reason for your interest?"

"In the past week a congressman in the United States has been murdered."

"Ah, Congressman Shapply. Yes, we know about him. He had business interests here in Barbados."

"This is a long shot, but we have some reason to believe that his death may have something to do with the death of Margarite Haller."

"Twenty years ago? And you now believe that the incident this afternoon may be related?"

"I said it's a long shot. And I have no idea what the connection might be. But if you can put us in touch with anyone who was involved with the case it may help."

"If you were an officer of the law there would be no question that we would help you. Being that you are a member of the press, it could pose a problem if the case is protected. However, let me see what I can do." He stood up from his desk and it was apparent the interview was over. "Gentlemen, I will be in touch if I can gather any information. If you need our services for any other reason, please, don't hesitate to call us."

They walked across the street to a small grassy park where Dave sat in a dirty yellow van with rusted-out rocker panels. He opened the doors and they climbed in.

"My cousin says I can use this until I decide what to do. Got wheels for a couple of days."

"Take the potholes easy, Dave. Mick here is gonna feel every bounce of this bus."

The medication from the emergency room left him groggy but did little to stop the sharp, stabbing jolts of pain on the trip back to the hotel. There was no sign of permanent damage to the arm. Some slight swelling where the skin was slightly burned, and a cut that they stitched up made the area sore to the touch and the strained tendons would take their own sweet time to heal, but he could use the arm, and he was alive. The van rumbled and bounced its way back to the hotel and Dave dropped them off at the entrance.

"Why don't you get yourself a little rest." T-Beau helped him out of the vehicle. "See how you feel in a couple of hours. There are some beautiful women here, help take our mind off our problems. Be a shame if we had to miss some of the finer points of this island."

Sever gave him a weak smile. "Jesus! I'm still shook up, and you're thinking of the women? Too many women, too little time?"

They walked to their rooms. "Somethin' I never tire of, Mick. A fine woman. Her company, her laugh, the smooth skin, the smell of her hair . . ."

"You never satisfy the hunger."

"You get some rest."

Sever walked in the room. Lie down for just a minute, then call Ginny. See how things were going back in the States. He closed his eyes. The minute stretched into hours.

Chapter Thirty-six

The phone was ringing. He struggled to sit up, wondering what he'd had to drink, or smoke, or ingest. He could remember nothing. The phone kept up its shrill, irritating ring. Oh, the painkiller. He was reminded as his shoulder throbbed. He picked up the receiver. "Yeah?"

"Gettin' to be dinnertime. Got a great spot picked out. We can get some good food, check out some local action, and go from there."

Sever was quiet. It took time to process the information. The medication messed with his brain waves but did nothing to stop the pain.

"Mick?"

"Sorry, Beau. I'm still a little foggy. I've got to clear my head and call Ginny. Can't lose sight of why I'm here."

"Alright. I'll call you in half an hour. See how you feel. You take care of yourself. We got a big day ahead of us tomorrow."

Sever called Ginny's room but the line was busy. The new guy? He left a voice message and leaned back on the bed. He tried to put his arms behind his head but the pain was too intense. No more pills. For some fresh air he walked down to the pool bar and ordered a double Scotch and soda. The bartender slid it across the bar without looking up, flirting with two bikini-clad tourists who could have been his daughters. Sever signed the tab and went back to the room. The phone was ringing as he walked in.

"Mick."

"Ginny."

"Are you all right?"

"Why?"

"I don't know. I just had a feeling."

"As a matter of fact. . . "

"I knew something was going to happen. I knew it."

He described the incident.

"Alicia Shapply," she said. "It's got to be. But why?"

"I don't know, but we're working two angles. We may be able to get the police involved. And we're still going to visit the recording studio. We passed on seeing Bobby Jergan today."

"Jamie sends his love."

"Not happy?"

"I think he'd like to see some progress in the story."

Sever sipped the Scotch, the double dose taking some of the sting out of his arm. "Assure him I'm collecting plenty of material."

"But, dude . . ."

"Yeah. I hear you. What else?"

"I saw Nick."

"And?"

"You're right. He had nothing to do with it. God, Mick, it was like old times. I was ready to take his head off, and then he turned on that Nicky Brand charm. He melted me."

Sever refused to take the bait.

"I'm convinced he didn't do it." A voice in the background spoke words Sever couldn't make out.

"Is someone in the room with you?"

"No. The news."

"And you're convinced . . ."

"I'm convinced he didn't have a thing to do with the murder. He's as confused as we are. Maybe more so. And I'm also convinced that he is very upset about what happened between the two of you."

"Yeah. I got that impression, too. I don't know, Ginny. I suppose if this situation ever shakes out, he and I need to have a heart-to-heart and air it all out."

"You should. After all, how many friends do you make in a lifetime? Anyway, he wishes you luck on your trip. He hopes you'll find a link to the killing."

"I'm sure he does."

She was quiet, the news background fading in and out.

"No more calls from the Ice Maiden?"

"No. If you want my opinion she's found a more direct way to tell you to stay out of her affairs. Jesus, a firebomb?"

"Beau agrees. He's sure she set up the incident on the road."

Sever took another sip of Scotch. The smoky liquid burned the back of his throat and he felt it course through his veins. The dull pain in the arm was almost gone. Better than the damned painkillers.

"I think so. It's hard to say. He's scared and he said to wish you luck on your trip. He seems certain you'll find some link to the killing."

"I hope I do. It's not going together well at all."

"You're used to the pieces going together like a jigsaw puzzle. In a murder like this, maybe they . . . listen, Mick. I shouldn't tell you this because you'll just worry."

"What?"

"I don't think it's serious, but someone is following me."

"The guy with the greasy hair?"

"No. It's been like, three times I've seen him. Either he doesn't care that I know, or he's bad at tailing."

"What does he look like?"

"Like the other guy you described. He's got his hair done in a marine buzz cut and he wears this tan trench coat."

"Ginny. Seriously. Take the first plane back to Chicago. This is stupid."

"I told you, I think he's harmless."

"He's got a gun in his pocket. I've seen it, sweetheart. Walk away from this."

She was silent.

"Ginny? Get the hell out of there. Now!"

Nothing. He could hear the voices in the background but couldn't make out the words.

"Ginny?"

"Oh, Jesus!"

"What? Ginny?"

"Oh my God."

"Ginny, what the fuck is going on?"

"The news. Chilli D tried to hang himself. I don't know if he's alive or dead."

Chapter Thirty-seven

I should fly back, man." T-Beau sat staring intently at the black water that lapped the shore.

"Yeah, I thought the same thing, but Beau, he's in the hospital. They've got a twenty-four-hour watch on him, and chances are you won't even get close to him."

"Yeah. You're right. Maybe I can do more good over here right now. We got people to see. Tomorrow should be very interesting. Still, I should talk to the boy."

Night birds called, the sound lingering on the evening breeze. They could hear the tinkle of cocktail glasses and dinnerware from the open-air restaurant twenty feet away. Sever licked the salt from his margarita glass and set it down on the sand beside him. "What do you think he's going to say?"

"Don't look good for him, does it? Shit, Mick, a man doesn't try to kill himself if he's innocent."

"Maybe the pressure got to him. And if he had killed himself, what would have happened to Nick?"

"Whole thing is one big mess."

"Beau, what's your stake in all this? You've got other artists. You've still got a career. Why such an interest in this guy? He's been up for murder before, struggling to make a comeback. Is it worth this?"

"Chill and me, we matched. You know what I'm sayin'? Sat down and did the talk and walked away as friends. I can't tell you what makes it special, but I like the man and he likes me. You stick with your friends 'cause in the end that's all you got."

"In the end, all you've got is yourself."

"One lonely man's opinion."

They were silent after that. Somewhere down the beach a girl laughed. Someone was strumming an acoustical guitar, the feint rhythmic ringing of the strings floating on the breeze. An island song. They sipped their drinks and looked into the darkness dotted with the lights of distant ships and stars. Minutes passed.

"Tomorrow we see Bobby Jergan." T-Beau lit a cigar, the flame from his lighter flickering in the air. He rolled the cigar, evenly lighting the tobacco, then reached into his shirt pocket and handed one to Sever. "This Jergan, he's a crook. He's used this island like a housewife uses the corner Laundromat. He took the money that Shapply scammed from people like you, and he invested it for him. Bought politicians, property, some sugarcane fields, and this recording studio. That's where all your money went, friend. And this studio, when I was here it was first class. They actually had some hit records so they became somewhat legit. And on top of that, the man used it as a front for dealing drugs. Maybe he still does."

Sever listened to the guitar down the beach. A peaceful,

lulling sound in a stressful, frantic environment. "So Jergan was able to buy off politicians and run his little fiefdom without interference from the law?"

"Pretty much. He was funneling money just about anywhere he had to. And these people were just like they are back home. Maybe worse. That money under the table is tax free, baby!"

"Life isn't all crooks, murderers, rappers, attempted suicides, and people threatening everyone from their girlfriends to their mothers." Sever lit the cigar.

"No. Sometimes life is just like this." T-Beau laughed.

"So fuck 'em. Let's stay here and not go back. Who's to say what the real world is. It may as well be this." Sever let the sweet smoke escape from his mouth.

"*This*"—T-Beau gestured with his cigar—"is where Bobby Jergan lives. Where a little girl was murdered. Where maybe there's an answer to Nick Brand's innocence or guilt. This may be the place where we find out why Chill tried to kill himself."

"Oh, yeah, there's that. So there is no perfect world?"

"The world is what you make it, bro'."

"Excuse me." The young waitress from the afternoon touched his shoulder. "I was checking out and just wondered if—"

"Any other night." Sever smiled at her. "We had a rough day. I'm afraid we're both a little down." He glanced at T-Beau. Surprisingly the large man nodded.

The girl frowned. "I'm sorry. Maybe tomorrow?"

"Sure. We'll see how things work out."

"I could show you the island. There's a great music club just down the road. Great music and lots of kids. Maybe we could go there?"

"Let's talk tomorrow."

"Tomorrow." She nodded and walked away.

Lots of *kids*? Sever sucked on the cigar. "Hey nineteen, we can't dance together, we can't talk at all." Steely Dan had put the age difference to music. Sever understood only too well. He was getting too old for this shit. Too old for all of it.

"Beau? Who's the guy with the buzz cut and the gun in his pocket?" Sever looked him dead in the eye. T-Beau blinked.

"The guy who pulled the gun on you?"

"You know that's who I'm talking about."

T-Beau looked away, watching the girl in the distance. "How the hell would I know?"

"He's following Ginny, and if she gets hurt, I'm going to find out who the hell he is. I promise you, I'll find out."

T-Beau frowned. He stretched and eased out of the beach chair. "I think maybe you're feelin' the effects of that medication, Mick. Anyway, I got some things to think about. Think I'll take a walk. See you tomorrow morning." He nodded at Sever and started down the beach. Sever lost him in the dark.

Chapter Thirty-eight

Billows of dust followed the borrowed van as Dave drove down the dirt road. Sugarcane rose up on either side, deep green and cornrowed. A Third World crop, over-produced, overpriced, and of major importance to the island. Dave swerved to avoid the large crater in the road and ended up hitting the smaller crater. The van shook and Sever grabbed his shoulder. At least the pain in his knee had subsided.

"Got a lead on a used van. Mon's gonna let me rent it by the month. If business picks up a little, maybe I can afford it."

"So what are we gonna do once we get there?" T-Beau stared out the window at the passing scenery. There was no mention of last night's tension between the two men.

"I'm going to ask him what happened on the beach that night. It seems to me that the whole purpose of this trip is to find out about that little girl."

"Got some great memories of the Caribbean, Mick. St.

Barts, Jamaica, St. Croix, the Bahamas, and even Havana. But Barbados was a mystery. Beautiful women, rum drinks like nowhere else, and music everywhere. But somewhere deep inside, I knew this was not a good place to be. It's shallow. No depth, no spirit. It's like an island with very little history. Hell, when the English found it nobody lived here. 'Cept pirates."

"Pirates." Dave muttered. "Whole friggin' island talks about pirates. Someone steals from someone else, don't be too harsh. The island has a history of pirates. Someone smuggles drugs in or out of Barbados, it's just part of our culture. Pirates. It becomes the excuse for behavior. Sons of bitches yesterday tried to steal my livelihood. Nothin' but pirates."

Sever watched the dust trail, trying to see if a second trail followed. There didn't appear to be anyone behind them.

"We'll be there in a couple of minutes. I'll wait in the van. Find some cool shade trees and stay out of the heat."

Dave pulled into the parking lot beside a model of car Sever didn't recognize. They stepped out into the hot sun and walked toward the nearest building. Sever pushed open the heavy wooden door and they entered a small reception area. No one was there. They waited for a minute, then Sever nodded to the hallway beyond and they walked down the corridor. The hall opened into a studio, with a mixing console and chairs and sofas scattered about.

"Place hasn't changed." T-Beau looked around. "New mixing board. 'Bout it."

Sever took in the room. The mixing board, the furniture, and a glass wall. Through the wall he could see microphones on stands, a drum kit, and a white baby grand piano. The room appeared to be ready for a session.

"Back then most of the acts here was local. Recent times

a bunch of British and American acts been recordin' on the island. Over at Eddie Grant's studio the Stones did *Voodoo Lounge*, and Sting and some other big-name acts put out some pretty good shit. Here at Bobby's studio, Bad Boys, the Noise, and Who's Your Mother?" T-Beau studied the mixing board. "Got some damned fine equipment here. Damned fine!"

"I didn't know I had company." The voice startled Sever.

"And you're Bobby?"

"I'm Bobby." He glanced over at T-Beau and seemed to stiffen. "Beau, how the hell are you? You're still hangin' around, eh?"

T-Beau looked up from the board. The balding white man wore a pair of large-framed glasses. His khaki shorts, white polo shirt, and sandals completed the ensemble. "Hey, Bobby."

"I haven't seen you since . . ."

"Since I recorded backup with the Rum Runners."

"Sure. That was it." He took off the glasses and wiped the lenses on his shirt. "Who's your friend?"

"This is Mick. Mick Sever. He's got some questions for you."

"What?" Bobby Jergan appeared to be somewhat concerned.

"You were a business partner with Robert Shapply."

"Yeah. He was killed in the last couple of days. This is about Shapply?" He watched them warily, his eyes shifting between the two men.

Sever motioned to T-Beau, pointing to the long leather couch. The big black man sat down on the sofa. "Sort of. I'm really here because of Margarite Haller."

Jergan was quiet, a blank expression on his face.

"Do you remember the name?"

Jergan sat down on a stool by the mixing console. He spun around on the rotating seat and faced Sever. "Sure."

Sever walked over to the board. "Bobby, some people back in the States seem to think you know something more about her death than you've shared."

The balding man smiled. "You've been talking to Shapply's kid. Well, here's what I know about Margarite Haller. I can tell you she was a cute little shit. Kind of flirtatious. You know, looked pretty good for a kid. Was startin' to fill out. We all had a picnic on the beach and she wandered away. They found her the next day. The police over here worked overtime on that one. The Shapplys pressed hard to get a conviction."

"A conviction? They had a suspect?"

"Oh, yeah. Guy who watched the kids while Shapply and his wife were off doin' whatever. Kind of like their nanny. Guy named Phillip Teese."

Sever glanced at T-Beau. "She never said a word about him being a suspect."

Jergan nodded. "Oh yeah. Number-one suspect. Hell, he was with those kids morning, noon, and night for a week and everyone kind of figured that he decided to nail the Haller kid."

"She was raped?"

"For a reporter you don't have a whole lot of information, do you?"

"This is how I get it, Bobby. Talking to people like you."

"She was raped. Then somebody bashed her head onto a rock. Put her through a bunch of shit."

"Anything else?"

"If someone thinks I'm holding back, let 'em come and talk to me. That's all I know. I don't know who did it and I don't have any thoughts about it."

"You and Robert Shapply, you got along together?"

"Hell, yes. He funded the studio, I ran it. We split everything down the middle."

"He did have a reputation for . . ."

"Screwing business partners? Yeah, and so do half the businesspeople in this world. Shapply was always straight up with me."

Once more Sever looked around the studio. "Shapply's money built this little enterprise?"

"Yeah. I guess you could say that. I was his partner. I had a lot to do with the profitability."

"That's what I understand." Sever walked to the huge slanted glass window with the view into the studio. "Were you here when the congressman was killed?"

"Hell, yes. Is that what this is about?"

"Supposedly the congressman was going to give the recording industry a black eye. Seems to me you might be someone who would have wanted him out of the way."

"Christ! Let me tell you something. And if you repeat this, I'll fucking deny I ever said it. Listen to me." Jergan was standing, waiving his finger, his voice raised about fifty decibels. "Robert Shapply never changed. I don't care what his prissy little wife says, I don't care what the righteous Reverend Joseph Evans says. The son of a bitch was using his position in Washington the same way he used everything else. To build more power, to make more money. It's the only thing Robert Shapply knew how to do! So don't be thinking that this man had a change of heart. He only did what worked best for him."

He sat down, spent. The energy seemed to drain from his body.

"Got a group coming in?"

"Yeah." His face lit up. "Three girls. They sing pretty good, a little jazz harmony thing with a calypso beat. Knock your eyes out, these three. The youngest is fifteen. Looks a whole lot older. We dress 'em right, give 'em some stage direction, and they've got major potential. Especially that young one. If she was a couple of years older . . ."

T-Beau stood up from the couch. "You ready to leave? I think I heard about enough."

Chapter Thirty-nine

The hell with this Phillip Teese." T-Beau watched the girl in a thong and no top jiggle down the beach. "Hell, I'd be lookin at Jergan! Slimy son of a bitch. Obviously he's got a thing for younger girls."

"Do you remember anything in his past about him liking younger girls? Is he married? Have a girlfriend?"

"Shit, there was lots of young girls hangin' around. Always are. You know that. Tryin' to look twenty-five when they're fifteen. Got lots of guys in trouble. Chuck Berry, Jerry Lee Lewis and his thirteen-year-old cousin, Steven Tyler, hell, R. Kelly had to get a marriage annulled from a sixteen-year-old not too long ago. Man believed he could fly. Tell me you were never tempted while you were hangin' with the bands."

"Elvis?"

"Yeah, even the King. What was Priscilla? Twelve?"

"A little older than that. Still, Jergan sounds like a pervert."

"He could do 'em two at a time with the best. Rock and roll, Mick. Sex is just a part of it."

"Okay. What about Shapply?"

"What about the man?"

"Did he mess around with younger girls?"

"The old man was a suit. And his old lady and kid were here."

"What? You think that makes him immune?"

"Mick, why don't you call Ginny. We'll see what the status of Chilli is."

They walked silently back to the room.

"Hi, babe. How did the interview go?" Ginny smiled a couple of thousand miles away.

"We found out there was a suspect. Guy named Phillip Teese. He was the baby-sitter, but I still don't see how it ties in with Shapply's death."

"Cops going to give you files?"

"So far, no. I'm confident, though."

"Mick, day after tomorrow I'm out of here."

"Yeah."

"They've got Chilli in a hospital room with round-the-clock guards. No one can see him. There are some stories floating around, but nothing I can substantiate. I'm sort of at a standstill back here."

Sever sat up on the edge of the bed. T-Beau sat on the patio, stuffed into a lounge chair, sipping a vodka and grapefruit, and staring out at the pool and the blue ocean water beyond. Sparkling, shimmering, crystal-clear water. Nothing else in Sever's life seemed as clear.

"Someone told the cops that Chilli said his debt would be forgiven if he'd kill the congressman." Ginny gave a sigh.

"Yeah, I know. So Nick's in jail because of that statement."

"And because they found the gun."

A sound track thundered inside Sever's head. Literally, he could hear the roaring background of strings, guitars, and percussion. The wind had picked up, and sun worshipers were picking up their blankets and heading for the safety of the pool or their rooms. From the balcony he could see palm trees bending in the wind.

"And that's why he tried to commit suicide?"

"They're not sure he did."

"What?"

"I told you, there are some stories floating around. One of them is that someone tried to kill him."

"Kill him?"

T-Beau looked back at Sever, raised his large body from the chair, and walked to the doorway. He looked questioningly at Sever.

"Kill him. The story is that he was drugged and someone tired to hang him in the cell. It's only a story, Mick."

"Hell of a story." The roar increased. He wished T-Beau would come in off the porch so he could close the sliding glass doors.

"Jamie says hi. He says please, please, please, call him."

"I will. I probably should give him something. Ginny, what about the guy with the buzz cut?"

"I called the cops."

"Jesus. It's that bad?"

"He's out there. I saw him five minutes ago. He stares at me."

"I need to get the hell back there."

"There is nothing you can do. Don't always try to be the protector. I figured, why take chances. But the cops said there's nothing much they can do until he does something."

"And you're not worried?"

"Maybe just a little. What I really need to do is get the hell back to Chicago. Do your work and get back here to spell me, okay?"

He drew a deep breath.

"Say hi to Beau, and you guys behave yourselves."

The line went dead.

"What?"

"It's a rumor, Beau. Only a rumor. Somebody tried to kill Chilli."

"Kill him? In jail?"

"I'm not there. I can't give you an answer."

"Shit, Mick. Maybe we need to get back there and see for ourselves."

"For a number of reasons I agree with you, but I seriously don't believe the answer is back home. Over here we can find another piece of the puzzle."

Chapter Forty

Phillip Teese lived in a small clapboard house set up on cement blocks along a row of similarly faded, dilapidated homes. Hot, bright Caribbean sun had bleached the boards almost white, like bones on a desert, and the dry wood had shrunk and cracked, leaving gaps that you could put your fist through. Dave dropped him off in the borrowed van and parked farther down the road, finding the one large shade tree on the entire street where he could cool off.

If Teese wasn't home he didn't know what he'd do. He had to finish the interviews, not just to get the story, but now it seemed to be important for Nick's sake. Sever stepped on the creaking porch and felt the boards sink slightly beneath his deck shoes.

An old white-haired black lady in a housedress and apron answered the door. She grinned at him, then leaned to the right and spit a wad of something dark and brown into the street.

"Sorry. Can't talk with tobacco in my mouth." Her speech was thick and her voice raspy. She grinned again, exposing her yellow- and brown-stained teeth. "What kin I do for you?"

"Is this the home of Phillip Teese?"

"It is. Yes." She kept the grin but made no effort to call for Teese or volunteer any more information.

After a moment Sever asked, "Is he home?"

"I'll have Phillip come out here. The house is not really ready for company." She stepped back and slammed the screen door in his face. He could have stepped through the large holes in the rusty metal screen.

Two or three minutes went by, and Sever could feel the heat and humidity plaster his clothes to his body. Sweat dotted his face and he wiped at it with the back of his hand. He knocked on the door again. An old man in a dirty undershirt and khaki slacks answered.

"Are you Phillip Teese?"

"Yes."

"I had asked the lady if I could speak with you . . ."

"Ah, she has a memory problem. Can't remember anything more than a minute. She can tell you what happened forty years ago, the exact day, hour, and minute, but she can't remember what she said sixty seconds ago." He shook his head back and forth, reminding Sever of a hound dog. "What can I do for you?"

"I'm Mick Sever. I'm a reporter from the States. I need some information about a picnic on the beach, twenty years ago."

The old man wrinkled his forehead. A sadness seemed to wash over his features and his eyes searched Sever's, pleading with him not to go there. Maybe it was Sever's imagination, but he could feel the old man's pain.

"Do you mind if I ask you some questions?"

His shoulders slumped and he eased himself down, sitting on the edge of the porch, his bare feet grazing the dusty road. He motioned for Sever to sit.

"You were in charge of the girls?"

"Yes. And at first it seemed like not much responsibility. They were good girls, well behaved. You see, I was a schoolteacher for a time. I'm used to taking care of children. And the two girls were used to having someone watch them so there was no adjustment. Besides, Mr. Shapply spent time with the girls also."

"Mr. Shapply?"

"He'd often take one or both of them to the studio to watch the bands record."

Sever had a hard time picturing Shapply entertaining the girls.

"Can you talk about that night?"

"I'd rather not. There was more responsibility than I should have been handed. No one told me that little girls could be murdered."

The old lady opened the door and walked out onto the porch. "I thought I heard voices. You didn't tell me you had company. My, my. Let me get the two of you something to drink." She turned and reentered the house.

"Mr.?" He stared down the road where it rose with the hill and disappeared from view.

"Sever. Mick Sever. Phillip, I understand you were a prime suspect. The Shapplys were pushing to convict you."

The light seemed to go on in his eyes. "Oh, they did. They helped make my life a living hell."

"But here you are. No conviction."

"All right. I can tell you some things. I was given the evenin' off."

"So you weren't even there?"

"No. I only had to show up and make sure the girls got back to their room. The adults had some, well, some adult pleasures to indulge themselves in."

"Adult pleasures?"

"Some cocaine. Hashish. The band had a good supply. I believe Mr. Jergan had brought something, too, and they had decided to wait until the children were in bed."

"So you weren't there when Margarite wandered off?"

"I didn't see her wander off. I had taken a long walk on the beach that night, with a lady who was not my wife. It was a big mistake."

"You were a suspect in the murder. Did you introduce the lady you were with? Couldn't she provide testimony on your behalf?"

"Eventually I did. It almost ended my marriage." The man turned his head toward the house. "If I had not introduced her, I would have surely been put in jail."

The old lady walked out, the creaking boards of the porch giving her away. "Oh, my goodness. We have company. What are you two men talking about?"

"Nothing, dear."

"Nonsense. I heard you mention jail. The picnic on the beach and the young girl. That's what this is about? And the lady you walked the beach with that night, Natalie Comstock.

A very sad state of affairs. And it was an affair, wasn't it, Phillip?"

He was quiet. She sighed and walked back into the house. "She remembers the past very well," he said. "It's the present that escapes her."

"Phillip, Robert Shapply was murdered. His daughter seems to think that Margarite's death has something to do with his murder. Who do you think killed Margarite Haller?"

"Shapply? Murdered?" He stood up, looking down at Sever. "Perhaps you'd better leave."

"Who killed Margarite Haller?"

He gave Sever a hard look. "I don't know, Mr. Sever. I truly don't." He paused for a long time. "But I do know that there was an occasion when I encountered Mr. Shapply with someone other than his wife."

"Other than his wife?"

"He's dead. It doesn't really matter now, does it?"

"It might."

"He asked me to keep the secret."

Sever got to his feet. "Before or after he tried to have you thrown in jail?"

"Oh, after. When he found out I had an alibi, *and* that I knew he was carrying on with someone else, he offered to pay me."

"Offered?"

"All right. He paid me. Five thousand dollars American."

"What exactly did you see?"

"I've said far too much."

"Phillip, the man was murdered. If there's a connection here I need to know what it was."

"I saw him kissing the young Haller girl."

"You're certain? It wasn't a kiss on the cheek, a fatherly type kiss?"

"It was a five-thousand-dollar kiss, Mr. Sever, on a part of her body that a fatherly type person shouldn't see."

Chapter Forty-one

The phone was ringing when he walked in the room.

"Dude!"

"Jamie."

"Sorry to bother you." There was sarcasm in his voice. "I was hoping you'd be in. The guys need to know if we're getting anywhere. You probably know about the attempted suicide and all."

"I know."

"Well, are we going anywhere with this story?"

Sever took a deep breath. It had been a long day, and there was a pain right behind his eyes so he closed them. The pain diminished slightly. "Yeah. We are getting somewhere. It's a long story, Jamie. There's a connection to Shapply's murder here. Actually, I wasn't sure, but Beau and I got stopped by a couple of guys with a shotgun and they sent a message that we needed to quit looking for that connection."

"Holy shit. Are you alright?"

"I'm fine. Actually, I'm not fine. You might say I got in the line of fire."

"And shot at back here. Maybe you ought to back off, Mick. Christ, the last thing we need is for you to get killed while covering a story for us."

"Oh? Is it alright if I get killed on my own time?"

"You know what I'm sayin'."

"Jamie, give me some time. If this pans out, you'll have one hell of a story. Ginny's covering everything back there and—"

"She said she's leaving in two two days. When are you coming back?"

"I hope to hell we're coming back in the next couple of days."

"Can we get something? Hell, we're running the basics, but we're paying for the byline."

"Hold on." He lay the phone on the bedside table and sat down. His knee throbbed, his shoulder ached, and the throbbing in his head did not want to go away. He walked to the sink, put a filter pack in the coffee machine, poured in four cups of cold water, and picked the receiver back up. "Okay. I'll get you something. Tell the *guys* I'll have an update by tomorrow. I can e-mail it to you from here."

"Great! Absolutely great. That's what I needed to hear."

"In the meantime, you might want to look into buying a big life insurance policy."

"Is something going to happen to me?"

"I was thinking about you putting it on me. Who knows, it could be a nice retirement nest egg for you." Sever hung up the phone and poured himself a steaming cup of black coffee. Hot, bitter, and strong. The headache was gone in sixty seconds.

He stepped out onto the balcony, feeling the heat and humidity baking the day. Calypso music was playing down by the pool where two young men were swabbing the deck in their khaki shorts and shirts. Calypso music, not the Harry Belafonte music about banana boats, but political lyrics. Dave had said something about one calypso song that literally stopped the privatization of the beaches throughout the West Indies. "Don't Take My Beach, Jack" put the beaches back in the hands of the public. It was a powerful calypso song that put the politicians on notice. In this case, calypso music was a positive force.

The phone rang again. He ducked inside and picked up the receiver.

"Mr. Sever? This is John from the police department. It has been decided that you can review the files on the case of Margarite Haller."

"That's great. Thank you. When can I see them?"

"We have them here at the station, so any time you can be free. Of course, you must review them here."

"Certainly. I'll be there first thing in the morning."

He hung up and called Dave's number. Dave's *office* was about six blocks away. It consisted of a gray folding chair and a card table by the side of the road with a phone connected directly to a box fastened to a telephone pole. Sever wasn't sure it was legal, but it seemed to get the job done.

"Yah? This is Dave."

"Dave. It's Mick Sever. Do you still have the borrowed van?"

"Mick, I dropped you off five minutes ago. You know I do. Do you and the big guy need a ride?"

"We do. First thing in the morning."

"Well, Mick. I've got the Queen scheduled in the morning, Prince Charles for late afternoon, and the future king to be, William, in the evening. He wants to visit the hot spots. Other than that . . ."

"Lots of sarcasm."

"Mick, it's not like it was a year ago, okay? Things are a little slow right now. And all I have is a borrowed vehicle. Of course I'm available. Just tell me what you need."

"I need to visit the police station. Blow Prince William off, will you?"

"He'll be disappointed. Will T-Beau be with you? I've told a couple of lady friends that I would introduce them the next time he rode with me."

Sever couldn't help but smile. "I haven't called him yet. We'll see if he can rally for the cause. He's usually up for the ladies."

"So we'll be leaving early morning? Mr. Sever, you can move here permanently. I will drive for you twenty-four hours a day."

Sever poured himself a second cup of coffee and dialed T-Beau's room.

"Yeah?"

"Beau?"

"Hey, Mick."

"Are you up for a trip tomorrow morning?"

"That's why we're here."

"We're going to review the files on the Margarite Haller case, and, Beau, meet me at the bar in about fifteen minutes. I had a very interesting conversation with Phillip Teese. You won't believe what he had to say about Robert Shapply."

Chapter Forty-two

About one hundred pages were crammed into a cardboard file. Handwritten notes, double-spaced reports, sketches, and diagrams. There were transcribed interviews with witnesses, maps of the area where Margarite Haller had disappeared, and photographs of what Sever assumed must be the partygoers and the victim.

"How you wanna do this?" T-Beau asked.

"You take half. There's no other organized way that I can see. If you see something that jumps out, just let me know."

Confined to a small interrogation room, they divided the documents and settled down to a battle-scarred metal table. The hum of an electric clock on the wall and the shuffling of their papers was the only sound.

Sever started reading summations of what witnesses saw. Amber's recollection was noted.

Best friend Amber Shapply. Says they were toasting marshmallows in the fire. Margarite burned her tongue on marshmallow and walked away from the fire to find something to drink. She never returned. Amber Shapply remembers calling after her maybe five minutes later. She walked in the direction that the young girl had walked. Says she may have heard some muffled screams but the sound of the water and voices back at the party made it hard to be sure.

Amber Shapply says she cannot remember who was at the party and who wasn't. She searched for her mother, Alicia Shapply, but never was able to find her. Says half an hour later Phillip Teese, baby-sitter, came looking for her and asked where Margarite might be. He said it was time that the two girls turned in for the night. Teese has no accounting of his whereabouts prior to the disappearance.

Sever glanced up at T-Beau, who seemed lost in his reading. Sever gazed at the picture of the girl. A head shot of Margarite Haller, smiling, her hair tousled in a sexy sort of way. The second shot was taken on a beach. She wore a brief white bikini, and Sever had to admit that she was attractive. She looked much older than her years.

Alicia Shapply was next.

Alicia Shapply, mother of Amber. The first time she was aware of a problem was when her daughter asked her if she'd seen Margarite Haller. She did not notice if anyone from her party had been absent for any length of time.

He scanned some others. It seemed no one had noticed anything suspicious. Phillip Teese's interview was at the bottom of the pile.

Phillip Teese, charged by the Shapplys with watching the children. Itinerant sugarcane worker. Former schoolteacher. Shapplys hired him through an employment service. Mr. Teese was walking the beach. He could not account for his exact whereabouts at the time Margarite Haller walked away. He says he had asked permission from Alicia Shapply to leave the group until eleven o'clock when he would pick up the girls and escort them back to the hotel. Confirmed by Mrs. Shapply.

"Beau. Phillip Teese was walking on the beach when the girl disappeared. There's no mention here about being with another woman."

T-Beau grunted and kept on reading.

Sever flipped through the papers and saw Robert Shapply's interview summary.

Robert Shapply, businessman and father of Amber. Had walked back to the hotel to retrieve some paperwork to share with Mr. Robert "Bobby" Jergan. Jergan was not around when he returned. Several other people saw Mr. Shapply return. Mr. Shapply was not aware of any problems until much later in the evening.

T-Beau looked up and stroked his chin. "What are we gonna see here that they haven't seen the last twenty years?"

"Probably nothing. But if Teese is telling me the truth, Shapply might have been with Margarite."

"Robert Shapply was gone about the same time. Teese didn't accuse Shapply of the murder, did he? The man might have been messing around, but that's a far cry from murder. And half of these people didn't notice who was there and who wasn't. It could have been anyone." T-Beau put down the paper he was reading. "And I'm tellin' you that Bobby Jergan and Robert Shapply were payin' off the local gendarme, so you can't believe anything you read here."

"Alicia Shapply and Bobby Jergan both disappeared for a while, too."

"Coulda been just lookin' for a place to take a leak."

Shuffling through the papers, Sever pulled out the sheet with Amber's summation. "Wait a minute. Amber Shapply says she couldn't find her mother."

"Uh-uh. 'Cause she was off in the trees."

"But right here Alicia Shapply says Amber asked her if she'd seen Margarite Haller."

"Somebody's lyin'." T-Beau shrugged.

"Somebody. Then when Robert Shapply comes back from wherever he was, he says he can't find Jergan. Nowhere in sight."

"Bunch of people havin' a party somewhere else."

"Let me find Jergan's summation. Here. *'Robert "Bobby" Jergan. Says he was having a conversation with Alicia Shapply. Left early and was in his room when the girl disappeared.'* "

"Yet Shapply says he was talking to Jergan and was bringin' back some papers for him to look at."

"Somebody is lying or, like you said, someone hushed it up." Sever put the papers back on the pile.

T-Beau frowned. "Alicia Shapply and Jergan . . ."

Sever held his hand up. "Can you picture that?"

"I don't know the lady, Mick, but Amber Shapply says that Bobby Jergan is holdin' somethin' back. That would be pretty big!"

Sever leaned back and stretched his leg, a twinge running up his thigh. "Alicia Shapply and Bobby Jergan go off together. Did they have a one-night stand?"

T-Beau ran a hand over his shaved head. "Or did they stumble on the murder? I'm betting that Jergan knew Shapply was having an affair with the Haller girl. Gettin' kind of warm in here."

"Time for a road trip?"

"I'm thinkin'."

"Let's find a phone and call Dave."

Chapter Forty-three

Happy to have the business, boys. Been a while since I had a couple of big tippers like you. Gonna need a bunch of you to pay for a new van." Dave did his best to miss the potholes, jerking the steering wheel and whipping the van back and forth over the bumpy road. "How's the shoulder?"

"Better. It only bothers me when I'm with you."

Dave laughed and swerved at the same time, avoiding a crater the size of Rhode Island. The dirt road was dusty and Sever could taste the grit in his mouth, grinding it with his teeth. Dave parked in the shade of a couple of evergreens, and Sever and T-Beau walked up to the studio. The same car was parked next to the building. This time, Jergan met them at the door.

"I was just headed out. It'll have to be some other time."

T-Beau gave him a hard stare. "It'll have to be now, Bobby. I want you to put on your thinkin' cap. Go back about twenty years to that little party on the beach."

Jergan pushed past the big man and T-Beau spun around, surprising Jergan and Sever with his speed and agility. He reached out and grabbed the balding man by the collar of his colorful shirt. "Let's talk, Bobby." He jerked him off the ground, the shirt collar threatening to tear.

"Okay. Jeez, put me down."

T-Beau kept him in the air. Sever couldn't believe the strength in the man's arm.

"Where did you and Mrs. Shapply go that night?"

"What?"

"Where did you two go? To get a little Caribbean delight?" He set Jergan down.

"*We* didn't go anywhere. I went to fucking bed." His face was beet red and he was shaking from either fear or anger. Jergan looked at T-Beau then back at Sever. "Jesus! Do you really think—"

"You tell us what happened." Sever nodded to T-Beau as he put the little man down.

"Let's go inside. I need to sit down for a minute." Stumbling with his first step, Jergan righted himself and opened the door. They followed him in, down the hallway and back to the studio. Jergan sat on the leather chair and Sever leaned up against the mixing console.

"First of all, I had nothing, absolutely nothing to do with the death of that little girl. You've got no right to start pushing me around."

T-Beau walked over to him, leaned down, and put a thick finger on his chest. "Suppose you tell us what happened!"

"Jesus. I've told you, I don't know what happened."

"There are people who think you do."

"Fuck 'em. I think Shapply knew what happened. I stayed out of it."

Sever's eyes widened. "Robert Shapply knew who killed the girl?"

"I can only tell you what the fuck I know, okay? And he told me he thought he knew why she was killed and who did it."

"Why are telling this now?"

"Because I want you two assholes out of here, and Shapply is dead. There's not a lot he can do to me now."

"What about Shapply's affair with Margarite Haller?" Sever watched for a reaction. He wasn't disappointed.

"Who told you that? Jesus, who told you that?"

"Was that why the girl was killed? Did you kill her to keep the affair quiet?"

"No. And I don't even know if there was an affair. They spent a lot of time together, but—"

"And the cops? They never heard this story?"

"You know, our studio venture was bringing in a lot of capital to this country. At that time they tended to look the other way when someone was paying the bills."

T-Beau sat down in a plush chair, sinking into the upholstery. "So they *were* paid off? That's what I always heard."

"Personally I still think the baby-sitter, Phillip Teese, had something to do with her death. I don't care about his so-called alibi. He had this strange wife and I wouldn't be a bit surprised if he wasn't looking for some strange. Little sexpot comes along like Margarite Haller and he gets tempted." Jergan pulled a cigarette from the pocket of his shorts and lit it with shaking hands. Gathering bravado from the nicotine, Jergan grew more defiant. "Who the hell appointed you as the police here? Why don't both of you just fuck off and get out of here?"

Sever glanced at T-Beau and motioned toward the door. "We're going, Bobby, but I need to find out who killed Margarite Haller."

"Get the fuck out of my life."

T-Beau and Sever walked down the hall and out the door into the oppressive heat.

"Shapply knew what happened."

"So does Jergan."

"You think?"

"I think."

"And we're not gonna shake it out of him. Damn!"

Sever shook his head. "Jergan and Shapply were putting money in and taking a hell of a lot out. And it sounds like they were watching each other's back. Pillage and rape. Like Dave said, it's a pirate culture."

"So, Mick. If Shapply knew who killed Margarite, maybe that's why he was killed. Doesn't sound like Chilli had a stake in this part of the story."

"Speaking of Chilli, let's get back to the hotel. I've got to call Ginny and see how that's playing out. Shit, if I could just buy about three more days from her."

"So she's leaving tomorrow?"

"That's what she says."

Dave pulled up to meet them and they drove down the narrow dirt road, throwing up more clouds of dirty brown dust. Five minutes later they pulled onto the pavement. T-Beau glanced back at the cloud of dust.

"Truck just pullin' in back there."

Sever looked over his shoulder and winced. He had to move slowly. "Lots of trucks over here."

"Could be our friends."

"I can't afford to have cousin's van set on fire, boys. Let's just go our own way," Dave said.

They passed a series of pristine white buildings gleaming in the sun with graceful palm-tree landscaping adorning the lush green lawns.

"Lots of money spent on them government buildings. The British embassy is up there." Dave motioned with his arm. "Many years ago I was in that building. I tended bar for a private banquet and served the Duke of Kent a beer. Imagine, me, servin' the Duke of Kent a beer." Dave turned his head and smiled at Sever.

T-Beau leaned over the passenger seat and looked at Sever. "Hell, I'd be more impressed if he served the Duke of Earl."

Dave stopped for gas and T-Beau bought a candy bar. "Got to keep up my strength."

The road meandered through a residential area with sun-bleached stucco houses, faded pinks and yellows and blues. The truck caught them unaware, racing past them in a second and disappearing around a curve a quarter of a mile ahead.

"Wild kids." Dave muttered under his breath.

"Dave." Sever watched the truck vanish. "Turn around. Go back to the studio."

T-Beau looked at him. "What the fuck?"

"That was the truck."

"Like you said, could have been anybody."

"I've got this feeling."

Dave pulled into a parking lot and turned the van around. He punched the gas and headed back down the road.

Chapter Forty-four

His car's still here. Man said he had to go somewhere." T-Beau eased his bulk out of the van and walked to the automobile. He glanced inside.

"Bobby Jergan is probably getting a little tired of us stopping in unannounced," Sever said.

"Well, let's get the right answer this time and we won't have to bother the man anymore."

"And let's find out why the fire-bombers were out here."

"Mick, I still say that could have been anybody's truck."

"I recognized the guy with the bottle, Beau."

They pushed open the door and walked down the hallway.

"Smells funky." T-Beau sniffed the air.

"Burned coffee?"

"Like somebody burned popcorn in the microwave."

They entered the studio, the long mixing board in front of them.

"Bobby!" Sever shouted his name. No answer.

T-Beau walked to the large glass window. "Jesus. Mick, there's our boy. In there."

Dark red blood stained the spattered back wall of the studio. Jergan's body lay on the carpeted floor, a smear of blood streaking behind him where he'd slid down the wall.

"Oh, my God. They must have put the barrel under his chin and . . ." Sever thought he might be sick. He turned away. He couldn't—didn't—want to. He suppressed the gag reflex.

"Shit. Nothin' left of the man's head, Mick."

Sever turned away. "Gunpowder."

"What?"

"That's what we smelled. Gunpowder."

"Man can't give us any answers now, can he?"

"I think that was the idea, Beau. He knew a hell of a lot more than we thought he did."

"Gasoline. Didn't smell that before."

Sever sniffed. "What?"

The walls shook with the blast, a wall of fire roaring through the doorway, down the short hallway, and exploding into the studio, throwing Sever to the floor. Somewhere he heard glass shattering as another explosion rocked the building.

He couldn't breathe. The choking black smoke smothered him as he crawled across the carpet. Pieces of ceiling rained down as he scrambled for the doorway, praying for a breath of fresh air. Through the smoke and flame he could see T-Beau, a dark motionless shape, five feet away. Sever's lungs ached, begging for a breath as he rose to his knees. He reached for T-Beau, grabbing the man's arm. Squinting into the thick haze he stumbled to his feet. His knee felt like it could give way at any second. With his good arm he pulled. Damn, the man was heavy. Slowly, Sever dragged him across the floor, staying low, inches at a time. The doorway was only a few feet away now. It was almost impossible.

He could make it out by himself. He knew he could get out alive, but probably couldn't live with himself if he did. Fuck it. He pulled harder, and ever so slowly the body moved. He could see daylight. The hot flames licked around him, but the smoke was the worst part of it. His slit eyes stung, and he could feel waves of heat wash over him as the flames climbed the curtains and started racing across the carpeted floor.

He stumbled and fell, rose again to his knees, and crawled, pulling with all his might. How long could you go without air? The black cloud parted and he struggled toward the opening. A short hallway and the door. He could feel the tears running down his cheeks. Either tears of agony or from the thick smoke that burned his eyes, nose, and mouth.

Pull once more. Tug again. Pull, pull, pull. He kicked at what remained of the charred door and it was over. He was out—barely. He grabbed a deep breath, tasting the heavy smoke and coughing it back out.

A figure appeared through the haze, coming at him on a run. There was no strength to fight. Sever collapsed on the ground as the man closed in.

Chapter Forty-five

He was coughing, choking, lying on his back. He raised his arm to wipe at his eyes and saw the clinging black soot that coated his hand and shirt. T-Beau. Where the hell was Beau? In the distance the fire raged, bright orange flames against a deep blue Barbados sky. Plumes of thick black smoke rose over the studio, a shroud to the bright sun above.

Sever slowly sat up. Palm trees, sugarcane in the field, a bright flower garden to his right, everything else was normal. Where was Beau?

"Mick. You okay?"

He gently turned. "Dave!"

"I thought I'd lost you two for sure. After you got free of the building, I pulled you out here. That T-Beau is one heavy son of a bitch."

"Is he alright?"

"Yeah. Over there. I had to blow some air down in his lungs, but he's fine."

T-Beau sat on the ground, his head hanging down. Sever gingerly stood up and walked over to him. "You going to live?"

He gave a deep sigh. "Sure. I quit hangin' with you I'll be fine."

"Hey. I saved your sorry ass."

"Yeah. Gotta thank you for that."

"What happened, Dave?"

"I'm parked over here," Dave motioned to the van, "just waiting for you, and the place goes boom."

"Our fire-bombers. They must have set a timer. When we got in there we found Bobby Jergan, his head blown off with a shotgun. Somebody decided to destroy the evidence."

"Damned good job of it," T-Beau said.

"Do you suppose the police are going to get a little tired of seeing us?"

T-Beau coughed, his voice raspy with the smoke. "I'm tired of this island, Mick. It's gettin' real close to goin'-home time."

Chapter Forty-six

They sipped ice-cold Banks beer and gazed out the window at the sunbathing tourists. Paradise for some.

Sever listened to the messages on the phone. Jamie wanted to know when he could expect the article. Shit! Ginny wanted to tell him that he'd better call while she was still there because she had to be leaving soon. The front desk, asking if he was checking out tomorrow as planned, and a call from the D.C. jail. The D.C. jail.

This call is from someone incarcerated at the Washington, D.C., jail. This call may be monitored. If you accept the charges please answer by saying yes. A click and a dial tone. Nick was reaching out.

Sever punched zero and the front desk answered.

"Can someone call here collect?"

"Certainly. You must clear it with the front desk, then we can put it on your credit card." The female voice was clipped and British.

"Consider it cleared," he said.

"Who's callin' collect?" T-Beau asked.

"D.C. jail."

"Everybody wants to be here."

He rang Ginny's hotel room. There was no answer and the hotel machine picked up. "Ginny. Nick tried to call. What's going on?" He hung up the phone and turned on the TV. A calypso band was playing, the soft rhythm and gentle sounds disguising the lyrics about a crooked politician who was out to fleece the locals.

T-Beau stared wistfully out the window, off the balcony to the palm trees and beach in the distance. Sever followed his gaze. "We're lucky to be alive."

"Ever been that close to death?"

"No." T-Beau stretched his tall frame. "Daddy died in a gang fight. Took a bullet in the brain."

"I didn't know that. And you still promote the music about gangstas."

"Not everybody's got an axe to grind, you know what I'm sayin'. I want to make music. Get people to reflect on what's happenin'. You know, maybe all this violence in music will get people to realize how senseless it can be."

"Do you really believe that?"

"Mick, music is a powerful motivator."

"It's what keeps me writing about it. Just when you think you've heard it all, something new happens."

"I was thinkin' about Dave's story," T-Beau said. "That song, 'Don't Take My Beach, Jack.' Powerful impact on keepin' all these beaches public."

"And then there's your music. People fall in love . . ."

"And *make* love."

The phone rang. Sever grabbed it and the voice recording started. He answered yes.

"This call may be monitored . . ."

"Mick?"

"Nick. Are you alright?"

"Yeah, I think so. I'm still here so things aren't going quite like I planned."

"You know I talked to Amber?"

"Ginny told me. So did Amber. And Ginny hasn't changed at all. Smart, good-looking, I should have taken her away from you when I had the chance."

"Fuck you. You didn't call to discuss my ex-wife." T-Beau nodded at Sever and walked out of the room.

"She said you had a serious accident?" Nick asked the question.

"A couple of them. T-Beau and I think Alicia set us up."

"Any reason?"

"Maybe." He hesitated. It had always been clear that Nick detested his mother and his stepdad, but Sever was hesitant. She *was* his mother.

"Mick?"

"Do you remember Bobby Jergan?"

"Sure. He was one of the congressman's partners. Ran the studio and other things in Barbados for the old man."

"He says Shapply knew who killed Margarite Haller."

It was Nick's turn to be silent. Finally he spoke. "And you think the congressman was killed because he knew? Well, I've got news for you, bro.' My little sister knows, too. Or she thinks she does."

"Damn. Somebody just blew Bobby Jergan's head off, about an hour ago, and then blew up the studio. I think it was done to keep *him* quiet."

"Oh, man. You're really steppin' in it. And you think my mother is behind all of this?"

"Somebody doesn't want the story on Margarite Haller to get out." Sever could hear Nick's heavy breathing on the other end.

"Man. She's a lot of things, but to have somebody killed?"

"It's only a guess, Nick."

"And, if I remember right, the little girl was raped. Could Jergan have been involved?"

"Nick, there's a story here that Shapply had an affair with Margarite Haller. It's pretty convincing. He paid off the babysitter to keep it quiet."

"What?"

"If it's true . . ."

"Mick. Aw, man. I hated the fucker, but having an affair with a thirteen-year-old?" Nobody spoke for half a minute. "My mother tried to kill you and my stepfather is a rapist? Makes a guy want to rethink his lineage."

"I can't prove any of it."

"Well, I got that goin' for me."

"And Jergan insinuated that the cops looked the other way about all of this. He said that he and Shapply were bringing in a lot of money, and—"

"And back then, a lot of drugs. The studio was a cover for that, too."

Sever sighed. "This just gets more and more complicated. Anyway, he says that the cops were, in effect, paid off."

"Listen. I called Amber. We had a long brother-sister talk."

"You talked to the boyfriend? Josh?"

"It only makes sense she picked a fucked-up boyfriend. Obviously, she came from a fucked-up family."

"So what did your sister have to say?"

"Like I told you," his voice sounded tired, "she said she thinks she knows who killed Margarite."

"After all these years?"

"She's told me some things she didn't tell you. She's certain she has this repressed memory and all that psychological bullshit."

"But, Nick, who killed Shapply?"

"With all your information, with all your suggestions about my mother and stepfather, I still think it was Chilli."

"Why?"

"He knew the old man was out to wreck his career. Kill the congressman, save his career."

"*And* he thought by killing Shapply, you would forgive the $250,000."

"Mick, I did not make a deal with Chilli. I did not tell him to knock off the old man and I'd forgive the debt. No way."

"Nick, listen to me. It makes no sense. If Chilli killed the congressman, he probably did it to save his career. That has nothing to do with Margarite Haller's death."

"Amber believes it does, and maybe Bobby Jergan believed it, too. She was very adamant about it."

Sever heard the door slam shut as T-Beau entered the room. He handed Sever another ice-cold Banks beer, the moisture dripping from the outside of the dark brown bottle. Sever tilted the bottle back, and took a long slow swallow. Nick wasn't allowed that pleasure.

"Man, I wish you could give me something to tie all this together."

"Mick, I'm trying. Amber says if you find out who killed Margarite, you'll find out why the old man was killed. She seems to think it's as clear as that."

"And I'm starting to wonder if all she wants is a twenty-year-old crime solved over here that has nothing to do with the killing of the congressman."

"Mick, if you've got any leads, please, follow 'em. I'm somewhat helpless at this point. Can you do me that favor? If the Ice Maiden is involved, it's worth a look, right?"

"All right. I've got a couple more things to check out and I'll be back." He gently put the phone down and reached down to massage his knee. After a shower and clean clothes he could still smell the smoke.

T-Beau was back on the patio, sipping his beer. "Friends are hard to come by, dawg. And even harder to keep. You know what I'm sayin'?"

"I don't know if Nick and I can ever be friends again, but the memory of a friend is like a good song, Beau. It stays with you."

He laughed, a low, rolling laugh from deep in his chest. "I do thank you for pulling me out of that hellhole. Got a debt to repay now. I will always be in your debt, Mick. Always. Always."

Chapter Forty-seven

He tried Ginny's room again but there was no answer. He could see T-Beau down by the shimmering pool, deep in conversation with a young British couple they'd met on the beach, a light-skinned black girl with a very brief bikini and curves in all the right places, and a pasty young white man wearing a white Speedo.

Staring at the blank screen he focused on a story line, then started to write.

> *Popular music, like any form of art, is meant to elicit a response. Although appreciation is a response, most popular music at its best strives to go much further. Love, lust, anxiety, hate, distrust and, in many cases, a physical response. Suicide, murder, rape, sex, have all been inspired by pop music—just as paintings, sculpture, and even tapestries have inspired the same acts over the centuries.*

The effect that art has on society was the subject of Congressman Robert Shapply's proposed congressional hearing.

Sever continued and five pages later copied what he'd written. He logged onto the Net through his phone and e-mailed the piece to Jamie Jordan. Clicking off the laptop, he clasped his hands behind his head. He closed his eyes and let his mind drift. Nick was getting restless and Ginny was leaving, going back to Chicago. T-Beau was ready to leave the island, and it was obvious Sever's support group was going to disappear very soon. He opened his eyes and gazed at the phone. He should call Ginny, but he really didn't want to deal with that right now. Maybe she wouldn't leave until she heard from him. Maybe. So he could fly back tomorrow and see her, convince her to stay a little longer. Hell, there was still something there. He'd known it on the carousel. He decided not to call. At least not right now.

The police told him there were no suspects in the murder and fire, and the case could be under investigation for months.

"Men like Mr. Jergan make many friends, and many enemies, on our island. Due to his financial success and business dealings it is not all together surprising that someone would do something like this."

Nothing else could be done on that front. So there was one more thing to do. He was nervous, tense, filled with pent-up frustration. Maybe it was Barbados, maybe it was the story and all of the loose ends, or maybe it was the idea that Ginny was going back to Chicago, back to someone who obviously had her attention. Or maybe it was that she hadn't gone back to Chicago, and someone was stalking her. He knew he didn't want to spend another twenty-four hours in Barbados. He picked up the phone and called Dave.

"Dave, you were going to rent a van. How much would you need to come up with to buy the van?

"Maybe eight thousand dollars, Mick. I'll come up with it somehow."

"I'll wire it to you tomorrow. You saved our lives, man. It's the least I can do."

It was time to go. The Barbados heat was getting to be unbearable.

Chapter Forty-eight

Sever walked down the corridor after clearing customs. He rented a car from the same clown at National and drove out to Amber's house. It was early enough and he hoped that the short-order cook was cooking and Amber was still home. He parked down the street and walked up the cracked sidewalk. T-Beau would be in Washington in another hour and maybe he could talk some sense into Ginny, asking her to stay and reconsider her obligations. He didn't want to go back knowing that she was in Chicago with somebody else. The thought of T-Beau and Buzz Cut interrupted his thoughts. If the man with the trench coat and gun *had* been coming out of T-Beau's room, how did T-Beau fit into the picture?

He knocked on the door and she opened it, looking somewhat bleary-eyed in a faded T-shirt and sweatpants.

"Oh, my God. What are you doing back here?"

"I think there are some things you left out of the story."

"You what?"

"You were anxious for me to go to Barbados. Your mom didn't want me there at all. I'm not sure why, and I'm not sure what *your* motive was for me to go."

"You talked to my brother, right? And it means nothing. I simply told him that I think Alicia and my father knew who the killer was. And my *father*"—she spit the word out—"he's not talking, is he?"

"Can I come in?"

"If you're going to badger me, no." She stood defiantly in the doorway, rubbing the sleepiness out of her eyes.

"I promise, no more badgering. I just want some answers."

"So do I, Mick. So do I."

She opened the door and led him through the strewn clothes and baby toys, past the playpen and a cheap plastic highchair.

"Sit down." She pulled a chair out from the kitchen table. "You tell me what you want to know. No bullshit, just questions and answers."

"Who killed Margarite?"

She was quiet.

"What happened to questions and answers?"

"I only answer if I know the answer. I'm not sure."

"Do you know who killed your father?"

"I can answer that. No."

Sever pushed the chair back and stood up. "Did you know your father was having an affair with your friend?"

Tears sprang to her eyes. She turned away from him, standing and grasping the table for support.

"You knew, didn't you?"

"Get out. I don't want you here." She was quietly sobbing.

"I'm sorry. But you knew, and you think somebody killed him to keep it quiet."

Amber walked to the door, holding it open, waiting for him to make his exit.

Sever traversed the obstacle course. "Amber. I think your father knew who killed Margarite, and he was killed. Bobby Jergan may have known who killed Margarite, and someone killed him. And you told your brother you knew who killed Margarite. Damn it. Don't wait for me to find the proof you want, because you may not live long enough to see it."

"Bobby Jergan?"

"Somebody blew his brains out. Literally."

"Oh, my God."

"Yeah. It wasn't pleasant. Look, you want me to figure this out because you can't. I think you know who the killer is, but you've finally got someone who will do the legwork for you and you're going to make me do it all. The questions are these. Who killed Margarite, and who killed your father?"

"You're being paid to find out who killed my father. I'm trying to find out who killed Margarite for the love of a friend who is long gone. You don't have a thing to lose, but I've got what's in here." She pounded her chest with her fist. Her voice grew louder, more intense. "You tell me, Mr. Sever, who has a stronger interest in the outcome?" Tears stained her cheeks, and she spun around and walked back toward the kitchen, leaving him to walk out by himself.

He wondered if she was right, or if his desire to revisit an old friendship was driving some of his search. Hell, he hated to think that friendship was going to compromise a really good story.

Chapter Forty-nine

Washington was cooler. Maybe it was the difference between the oppressive heat of Barbados, but it seemed more like fall than just a few days ago. He had the driver take him directly to the hotel. It was time for an update from T-Beau and Ginny.

He knocked on her door and she answered immediately, stepping back, surprised to see him.

"So you just show up? No phone call, nothing. I was worried sick about you. My God, you were almost killed." She was miffed.

"I thought maybe Beau talked to you."

"Oh, he did." She grabbed him by the neck, pulled him down, and kissed him full on the lips. "I'm glad you're back."

"Not as glad as I am." He gave her a broad smile.

"Someone else talked to me, too."

"Listen. I need to run some ideas by you. I want you to stay."

"Let's walk." Ginny pulled on a sleek black leather jacket and walked out the door, irritated that he wasn't following. "Come on, I feel like a walk!"

They went down the elevator in silence and walked out onto the sidewalk. She was two steps ahead of him and he quickened his pace.

"Alicia Shapply."

"Ginny, these stories—they're a lot easier to work through when you're here."

"She called me and we met for coffee. I thought it would be informative, and boy, was it!" Ginny was all business now, power-walking her way down the street.

"I want to hear about it, but first, let me say this. Just hear me out. I want you to hang in here a couple more days. I'll pay you whatever you need."

"She almost threatened me, Sever. Are you listening? She almost threatened me. And, she threatened you. You couldn't pull me off this story. Tell me to go home, and I'll tell you to go to hell. The lady pissed me off royally, and there is no way I'm leaving."

"What?"

"Have you listened at all?"

"Yeah, sort of. I had this speech. You threw me off."

"Well, listen now, buddy boy. The Ice Maiden told me to get off the case, and she suggested you do the same. She said our lives could be in danger, and I got the impression she was the danger."

"Was she specific?"

"You be the judge," Ginny said. "She started off saying she made a big mistake asking you to talk to Nick. Then she said you made a huge mistake talking to her daughter. And she followed it by saying you were probably sorry you'd gone. When I asked her what she was referring to, she said to ask you about your trip."

"So she almost admitted to setting me up?"

"I don't think that would stand up in court, but it was close. She said there were circumstances you could not possibly be aware of and to stay out of her life. She said, point-blank, life could become very unpleasant for you and for me."

"She said that? In those words?"

"Pretty damn close. Mick, if her husband had an affair with that little girl, Alicia Shapply is trying to stop the story from getting out. It would be a huge stain on her image and the family name."

"So what did you do?"

"I wanted to walk away."

"But . . ."

"I didn't. I decided to play it out. I remained calm."

"On the outside?" Sever grinned, picturing the scene.

"On the inside I was like molten lava. Ready to erupt. Damn, Mick. The lady has balls." They stopped for a light and Ginny nudged him.

"Over my left shoulder, standing by the brick wall."

Sever glanced back. The man's hand was cupped over his mouth, lighting a cigarette.

"Yeah?"

"That's my friend. Don't look again. Just keep walking, see if he follows."

Sever fought the urge to turn again. He felt a chill and wished he'd worn more than the pullover sweater.

"Are you sure?"

"It's him. Don't look. Just keep walking."

"We should find a cop."

"Oh. Do you see one hanging around?"

Sever hesitated. "So, you've arranged to stay?" He approached the question cautiously, afraid maybe he'd heard wrong.

"How much more emphatic do I have to be? I want to nail the bitch." She kept up the frantic pace.

"Nail her on what?"

"I don't know. But she needs to be brought down a peg." Ginny stopped and looked Sever directly in the eye. "I called Chicago. What are they going to do? Fire their best editor?"

Sever watched her eyes, filled with fire. He started to ask how other people might feel about her staying in Washington, but decided now was not the time to bring it up. Maybe never was a better time.

Ginny turned to Sever, but her eyes looked past him, down the sidewalk. "He's back about half a block."

Sever turned.

"I told you, don't look."

"The guy has a leather jacket. Are you sure—"

"I'm positive. There's a side street about two blocks up. We can go down there and see if he follows us. Just keep walking."

"The Phillip Teese story is huge. Shapply supposedly gave him five thousand dollars to be quiet."

"After Shapply almost got Teese convicted of murder."

"Once he found out Teese had an alibi, *and* after Teese admitted he'd seen Shapply in a compromising position, he changed his tune."

"Mick, you've been led to believe that whoever killed the little girl will know who killed Bob Shapply."

"Amber Shapply seems to think that's the case."

"But it still could be any one of them. Teese, Jergan, Alicia, the hotel manager . . ."

"Or someone else from the property. No one knows how many people were there, or when they left."

"What if it was Shapply himself? The congressman?" She appeared to drop something, bent over to pick it up, then continued her fast pace. "Our friend is about a block back."

Sever kept his gaze straight ahead. "I asked Amber point-blank."

"You asked that poor little girl if her father killed her best friend?"

"Yeah. I'm sure she knows they had an affair."

"Apparently Bobby Jergan knew it, too. And that's why he was killed?"

He shuddered. The image of Bobby Jergan's blood on the wall of the studio stayed with him.

"Mick? Are you alright?" She slowed down and gazed at his face.

"I think so."

"T-Beau said you saved his life." She stopped and touched his arm. "You could have been killed. I'm glad I didn't know until later. It's hard to think about you not coming back."

"Well, I am back. And I'd love to put this thing to rest."

"So, what about the congressman?"

"All Bobby Jergan said is that Shapply knew who killed the girl."

"And you think Jergan knew who killed her, too?"

"We'll never know."

"Jesus, Mick. They found the gun in Chilli's apartment. He had a motive. Why don't you just let it go?" She tugged and led him down the side street. He started to protest. The last time he'd taken the road less traveled, he'd been attacked.

Chapter Fifty

White-painted, two-story brick buildings lined the street. The sign in each dark window was hand-painted with flowing script to show the upscale nature of the development: *The Boulevard. A shopping community. Coming this fall.*

In smaller type the signs gave the phone number to call for more information. It was fall. The shops did not appear to be open.

Sever carefully looked over his shoulder. The pain was there, nothing else.

"Mick. He'll be along any second. There's a doorway up ahead." She motioned. "Hurry up."

"If it's Buzz Cut, he carries a gun. We really should think this through."

"Come on. If he was going to do something, he's had plenty of opportunity. He's been following me the entire time you were in Barbados."

He strained again to see over his shoulder. "You have no idea what these people are like."

She grabbed him by his good arm and pulled him into the alcove. "Up against the door. Flat. We don't want him to see us."

They stood still, Sever catching his breath. While he was cold minutes ago, he was now perspiring. He could feel rivulets of sweat running down his chest under the sweater. He pressed his back against the glass door, the cool exterior feeling good against his body.

"Mick, there's one more thing. I should have remembered to tell you but a lot has been going on. Charlie White. He did time for robbery."

Sever's voice was coarse, almost like a whisper. "I thought you said he was clean."

"I thought he was. Apparently the limo company missed it when they did a check, and so did I. Another state, about five years ago."

"Robbery? It's not murder."

"No. But there's more to it."

"What?"

"He . . ."

The sound of someone jogging, almost running, disrupted the conversation. Whoever it was paused at the corner. Sever could only imagine Buzz Cut looking this way and that, trying to figure out where the two had gone.

Now the steps fell slowly, deliberately. Sever could hear the sound of heavy breathing as the walker slowly approached. The guy sounded like he had a bad asthma attack.

Ginny gripped his arm, her fingers digging into the muscle. They stood like statues, Sever wondering what he was going to do. With one bad arm and one bad leg he wasn't a prime candidate to take out the stalker.

He strained to listen. A car backfired down the street and he felt her shudder. There were no more steps, there was no more wheezing. Nothing. The sound of traffic maybe a block away.

Sever put his hand against Ginny, keeping her pressed against the door. He leaned out of the doorway, looking toward the corner. There was no one in sight. He hesitated for a moment. No weapon, no defense whatsoever. Did he really want to meet this guy? He eased out slowly and walked to the corner. A woman with a scarf pulled over her head was pushing a shopping cart halfway up the other side of the street. There was no sign of anyone else.

"Ginny." She poked her head out. "He's gone."

"It was him, Mick. It's just unnerving, having someone right there every time you walk out the door."

"You've never seen the other guy again? The one who said he had something for me when I got home?"

"No. Just the guy with the marine haircut. I don't think he's dangerous."

"At this point I think everyone is dangerous. Even the people on our side." They walked slowly back up the street.

"Anyone particular?"

"Every one of them, Ginny. Every one of them."

Chapter Fifty-one

He was waiting for Sever in the lobby. This time he was dressed in a crewneck sweater and a pair of soft denim jeans.

"Mick. Good to see you!" He stood up and reached for Sever's hand.

"Reverend." Not quite the same enthusiasm. Someone else he wasn't sure about.

"It's Joseph, remember?"

Joseph, not Joe. Sever smiled.

"Sure. Joseph, this is Ginny."

The Reverend smiled broadly. "Ginny, so good to meet you. Mick, I was hoping we could have a short talk."

"About?"

"Current events, and my nephew. I've been to the jail to see him."

"And Chilli?"

"You heard about Chilli?" He gave Sever an inquisitive

look. "He tried to commit suicide, Mick. I think his past and present haunts him."

"How is he?"

"In the hospital. The doctors say he'll live, but there may be some damage to his throat. Not great for a man who makes a living with his voice."

"And Nick?"

"He needs a friend. I sincerely think you should visit him. He doesn't seem to be making much progress on getting bail." Evans motioned to the two overstuffed chairs in the lobby.

"You two talk," Ginny said. "I'll be in the room, Mick." She gave him a long look, but he couldn't read her thoughts.

"Rev—Joseph, did you know Chilli D the last time he was in prison?"

"I did. I had an occasion to work with him."

"You tried to get him to walk the straight and narrow?"

Evans chuckled. "I think my stand on rap artists is public knowledge. And God knows, Chilli D was one of the biggest offenders. We worked together for a short time. Things change."

"And the hearings that you were going to have . . ."

"*Still* going to have, Mick. I think we can make a strong case for those hearings."

"You are going after Chilli D."

"And Ludacris, and Snoop, and even your friend T-Beau."

Sever stared at him for a moment. "And your nephew?"

"Well, he's not a player in the true sense of the word. He's not on the front line like an artist, producer, or director. Nick is in the background, and I think we'll deal with the players first."

"What's in this for you?"

The Reverend gave him a quizzical smile. "The world will be a safer, better place."

"Nothing to do with your reputation? Your ministry? Your national image?"

Evans stood up, brushed at a spot of imaginary lint on his sweater, and gave Sever a broad smile. Sever hadn't really caught the glint of his deep green eyes before. The sparkle and the brilliant color surprised him. His eyes alone could win the hearts of converts.

"Mick, you above all people know about image. You know that I have a lot to gain. Certainly this will enhance my position, my 'national image,' as you refer to it." Joseph Evans looked down on Sever. "And if my national image is enhanced, look at the good I can do. Look at the people I can help, the causes I can stand up for. Mick, there are few people who can really change the world. Let us hope that those who can change the world, change it for the better." He reached down, clasped Sever's hand in his own, and walked out the door.

Chapter Fifty-two

Sever rang Ginny's room. Busy. Fucking busy. Sever thought about going to her room, but being sober, decided it wasn't a good idea. He'd ask about the phone call, she'd tell him it was the boyfriend, he'd bristle and . . . hell, he wished he were drunk.

He called T-Beau's room. No answer. What good were phones if no one was home? The laptop on the desk sat waiting, but he wasn't in the mood. He walked to the window and stared out, seeing a line of buildings in the distance. There were too many unanswered questions.

He spun around and headed out the door. It was time to confront T-Beau. Had Buzz Cut been in his hotel room and what was the connection?

No one answered the knock. He waited thirty seconds, hoping the big man was just taking his time opening the door. Finally he took the elevator to the lobby. The young man at the desk smiled.

"Can I help you?"

"Do you know if Tony Beauregard is in the hotel? Did he by any chance pass by here?"

"Mr. Beauregard is not in the hotel."

"Did he say where he might be going?"

"He checked out, sir. I don't believe he left a forwarding address."

"Checked out?"

"Yes, sir. Is there anything else I can do for you?"

"You're certain?"

"Yes, sir."

Sever gazed at the glass revolving door. Finally he headed up the elevator to his room. Right now he just wanted to lie down and forget about it all. He was suddenly very tired.

Chapter Fifty-three

The ringing in his ears confused him. Shaking his head, he sat up and stared at the clock on the television: 9 P.M. He struggled to put his thoughts together. Was it ringing in his ears, or was it the telephone by the bed?

Sever let his head drop, his chin hitting his chest. He struggled for consciousness. He was still dressed. He remembered just closing his eyes for a minute.

The phone rang. Sever blinked his eyes and grabbed the receiver. Maybe it was Beau.

"Mick?"

No answer.

"Mick. God damn it. Talk to me."

He ran his teeth over his tongue, scrapping off the film.

"Ginny?"

"Thank you for picking up!"

"I was . . ."

"Asleep. I can tell. I'm sorry I didn't call you earlier."

He slowly drifted into consciousness. She'd been on the phone *earlier*.

"Mick! God damn it, answer me."

"I'm here. What the hell is so important?"

"For whatever it's worth," she said, pausing, "are you still awake?"

"I'm awake, Jesus! What is so important?"

"I didn't get a chance to tell you. When Charlie White got out of jail for robbery, Joseph Evans helped get him his job."

Silence.

"Did you hear me?"

"Joseph?" He rubbed his tired eyes.

"Mick?"

"I'm here."

"You can be so distant."

"I'm a whole lot closer than you think I am."

"So what do you think?"

"You know every thought I have."

"How did Joseph get—"

"It's part of what he did. When ex-cons got out, Joseph had a network of people who helped get them a job. He was responsible for getting Charlie White the job with the limo company."

"Nothing wrong with that, except it didn't show up in the background check. Can anybody explain that?" He walked to the sink and splashed cold water on his face, shaking out the cobwebs.

Ginny was silent.

"Does it make any difference?" Sever dried his face with the heavy hotel towel.

"I don't know."

"So who killed the congressman?"

"It's still Chilli D who had the gun."

"We've got all these pieces. Now we have to solve the puzzle."

"Mick, I really was worried about you. It keeps coming to me that there was a chance you would never come back."

"I know."

"Do you have any wine?"

"Sure. In the minibar."

"Wanna open a bottle?"

"Am I getting company?"

"Unless you're really tired. You had an exhausting couple of days."

"I'm waking up."

"I'll be there in a minute."

Chapter Fifty-four

He'd forgotten about T-Beau. Not exactly forgotten, but there were other things on his mind at the moment. She rolled over and looked into his eyes, her blond hair fanning the pillow.

"Hey, that was nice."

"It was."

She raised up and kissed him, her tongue working its way into his mouth. Ginny pulled him closer so they were pressing tightly together. Her hand dropped down and she gently stroked him. "Here, let me get on top. You've done enough work tonight."

They fell into a familiar rhythm, and when she climaxed she cried tears and collapsed on his chest.

When he woke in the morning she was gone.

Chapter Fifty-five

Sever checked his messages again. Another message from Jamie. That was it. Nothing from T-Beau.

He called Ginny's room. The line was busy. He couldn't win. He dialed Jamie's cell phone.

"Mick? Man, we got some catching up to do."

"I sent you the article, Jamie."

"Come on, Mick. We're talking about a whole lot more than just an article here. I checked with the hotel in Barbados. They said someone tried to torch your taxi? And somebody shot at you?"

"Settle down. The shots were taken at somebody else. Jamie, this could take a while."

"I'm getting pressure, Mick. Can we meet somewhere?"

Sever glanced at his watch. Late morning and he was by himself. No Ginny, no T-Beau. "Sure. I owe you that much."

There was a sigh of relief on the other end. "Thanks, man. Why don't I stop by and pick you up?"

Going for a drive with the chain-smoking Jamie Jordan wasn't high on his list of priorities. His lungs still burned with the smoke from the studio fire. Plus, he wanted to see if he could pick up Buzz Cut again. This time he'd confront him and see exactly what the tail was all about. It was time for a little backbone.

"Let's walk. I need to get some fresh air."

"Sure, sure. There's a place at one of the entrances to Rock Creek Park." He described the location. "Shouldn't be more than a ten-minute walk or a couple of minutes by cab. How about half an hour?"

"Sure, Jamie." Now he had to decide how much to confess. If he told him everything, he might want to run with the story. Or he might think he'd wasted the company's money. Sever hated half-finished scenarios. He had a hat full of theories, suppositions, notions, and opinions, but nothing concrete. Again, there were a lot of pieces to the puzzle, but no solution.

The cab driver nodded as Sever left him a ten-dollar tip. There was no sign of Buzz Cut. He'd spent a couple of minutes in the hotel lobby, then another three or four minutes outside the hotel, waiting for a cab. He glanced around, half expecting to see the man lurking in the shadows.

Sever walked down the slope, the grassy meadow stretching out in front of him. The traffic noise disappeared behind him, the trees and landscaping absorbing the sound. The last clear sound he heard was the roar of a motorcycle as it passed. The throaty sound lingered in his ears as he entered the quiet, peaceful park.

Jamie was waiting. "Hey, dude! Let's walk, let's talk."

Sever bristled. "Jamie, I don't have the story. It's coming together, but so far, no luck."

"Mick. You know this business better than I do. And you know I'm under a hell of a lot of pressure from the top. We offered you a lot of money to cover this story and the boss wants your input. I don't care if you don't know shit. We need something." Jordan looked at Sever pleadingly. "What the hell happened in Barbados?"

They walked, the crisp red and yellow leaves crunching under their feet. Sever kicked at a small rock, sending it careening down an incline. He looked up into the towering foliage and saw the awesome display of gold- and copper-colored trees. There was nothing, absolutely nothing that Jamie Jordan could run with unless Sever gave him permission. He took a deep breath, feeling the fire in his chest.

"A thirteen-year-old girl was murdered in Barbados twenty years ago. Somebody went to a lot of trouble to stop me from asking questions about that killing."

"And what does that have to do with Shapply's murder?"

"I'll be damned if I know. But there's a link. Do you see why I'm reluctant to say anything at this time? Jesus, Jamie, if I laid it all out for you, you'd have the same question. Just let me finish with this."

"Finish? You haven't even started. I was hoping to get a story."

"Jamie, the congressman's daughter believes that whoever killed this girl may be involved in her father's death."

"Do you buy into that? I think there's a pretty good case that Chilli killed old man Shapply. I don't understand why you're not working that angle."

"Because T-Beau thinks it could be someone else."

"T-Beau?"

"Yeah. I wanted to believe that Nick Brand wasn't involved, and he wanted to believe that Chilli wasn't involved."

"And what do you believe now?" Jamie picked up a small branch and flung it into the trees.

Sever changed the subject, giving him a sidelong glance. "Have you had anyone following Ginny?"

Jamie paused. "Following?"

"Yeah. To see what she's doing, who she's talking to?"

"No. I wouldn't do that."

"As much as you want to keep tabs on what's going on?"

"I haven't had her followed. You're a professional, and so am I. I don't do things like that."

"Somebody's been following her. And me."

A green tractor pulling a three-deck mowing unit appeared from behind the trees. The driver sported a baseball cap and Sever could see he wore earphones, either to keep out the noise, or play his tunes. The way he was bopping from side to side, Sever assumed the man was listening to tunes. The tractor ran up an incline on the grassy area and the blades from the deck ground the fallen leaves into a powdery dust that seemed to linger over the meadow. The smell of fall was in the air.

"Is it safe to be around you?"

"I'm starting to wonder."

The tractor drove off behind a grove of trees, and the sound of the diesel engine faded. They continued their walk, silent now, birds and squirrels in a symphonic chatter and the distant rumble of traffic filtering through the forest. Sever heard the motorcycle from the street, its distinctive Harley sound as it pulled off and started down the path. He looked back but saw nothing.

"Jamie, you're right."

He seemed surprised. "I am? About what?"

"Maybe it's time to concentrate on Chilli. He had the gun. He's served time for murder. And, he's got a motive. He wanted the congressman out of the way so he could get on with his career. I'm making this thing way too hard."

"Are you going to see him?" Jordan asked.

The bike was closer, off to the right. The sound was coming from the grassy area, off the path now.

"Yeah. I think it's time."

The rider was heavy on the throttle, the throaty roar of the engine splitting the still air.

"He's still in the hospital, Mick. I read they've got three guards on him at all times."

The glint of chrome caught Sever's eye as the big bike careened around a cluster of shrubbery, the sun bouncing off the fender. The driver was dressed in black, wearing a shiny black helmet and full mirrored face shield.

"I'll get with his attorney and set it up."

The rider hit the brakes, the bike spinning in the grass and leaves like a skier who suddenly stops his forward motion. Freshly mown grass and leaves spat out from the rear tire as Sever watched him slip his hand into the pocket of his black leather jacket and pull out a black pistol. Everything was black.

"Mick, are you—" Sever hit Jordan low, a body slam that took him to the ground as the gun fired once, twice, three times. One more shot, the dirt kicking up in front of him.

Feeling the burning pain in his shoulder, he grabbed Jordan and rolled away from the shots, seeking shelter in a shallow ditch.

Sever heard the drone of the tractor, making its sweep down the incline. Another shot hit the tree behind him. The rider twisted the throttle and the bike roared, stuttering for just a moment, then rocketed up the hill and out of sight.

Sever glanced up, seeing the tractor in the distance, the driver still moving to the beat. Something was wet and warm on his hands. He looked down, suddenly hypnotized by the oozing red fluid flowing between his fingers. He couldn't feel any pain. He eased himself up to a sitting position and then saw the ragged hole in Jamie Jordan's chest. The blood-soaked shirt was plastered to his pale white skin.

"Jamie!"

No answer. Sever pulled his blue oxford cloth shirt off, ripping a button in the process. He pressed it tightly against the wound. Leaning close he listened for breathing, detecting a shallow raspy gasping from the man's open mouth. He ran toward the tractor, waving his arms but the driver was looking the other way. Sever sprinted into the grass, realizing he was slightly out of breath already. No time to think. He ran into the path of the tractor and the driver gave him a strange look, not knowing what to do about a shirtless man trying to hijack his vehicle. He finally came to a complete stop, glancing warily behind him to see if there were any reinforcements. He slipped the headphones off.

"Got a man who's been shot." Sever was gasping for air, pointing to the path. "Do you have a cell phone?"

"Yeah." The man was being cautious.

"Call the cops. Call park security and have someone get an ambulance. Right now."

The man pulled a phone from the clip on his belt and punched in a series of numbers. He spoke into the mouthpiece, then slipped it back into his belt. "Security wants to know if you got a gun."

"I didn't know it was a prerequisite for visiting the park."

The driver jumped off the tractor and looked around as if confused. "Is there anything we can do?"

"Wait," said Sever. "All we can do now is wait." He was still catching his breath as he trudged back up the incline to the shallow ditch on the other side of the path.

Chapter Fifty-six

God, Mick. That could have been you." Ginny was frowning as they left the hospital lobby and walked down the hall to the huge glass entrance doors.

"I'm sure that's not much conciliation to Jamie."

"He's tough. He'll survive."

"The doctor says it missed his heart by centimeters."

"What were you two doing in the park?"

"I needed some air, and I thought I'd see if I could spot your stalker."

"This sounds more serious than a stalker."

"You know where my will is?" Sever asked, tugging at the scrub's cotton shirt they'd given him at the hospital. It was short, tight, and uncomfortable as hell.

"Third drawer, study desk."

"Seriously. If something happens to me, don't forget. And maybe you should keep your distance, too." They stepped into the last rays of sunlight, fading on the horizon.

"No, you don't. I'm staying as close to this as I can get! I think the Ice Maiden had something to do with this, and by God I'm sticking around until we find out why she wants you out of the way."

Sever flagged a taxi, and they stepped in.

Ginny was quiet for a moment. She had that frown with the crease between her eyes and the furrowed brow.

"You're really upset about this."

"Upset? My God, Mick. You are . . ."

Sever waited. "I'm what?"

"You are," she said, still hesitating, "I don't know what you are. Either you're driven beyond what's good for you, or your ego tells you that you're invincible."

"I just want to put it together."

"Even though someone is gunning for you?"

"Maybe they were trying to get Jamie."

"And maybe Lee Harvey Oswald meant to kill John Connally. If the Ice Maiden wasn't responsible, who was?"

"T-Beau?"

Ginny's eyes were wide as she spun around and grabbed his arm. "What?"

The cab driver turned and gave them a quick glance.

"I think T-Beau may be involved."

"No!"

"Ginny, I think Beau is responsible for the guy who's tailing you."

"Mick, you're crazy."

"I don't think so. The guy with the buzz cut was walking down the hall outside T-Beau's room right after we were attacked on the street. I've thought it through. T-Beau's a biker, and I know a biker took a shot at me in the park."

"So? Maybe this guy was staying in the hotel. Maybe he followed you back and he was going to confront T-Beau. Walking in the hall is your evidence? There are thousands of bikers. Come on, Mick! Why don't you simply ask Beau?"

"He's checked out and nobody knows where he is."

The cab pulled up in front of the hotel.

"Do you want to know if T-Beau is involved?"

Sever opened the door and handed the driver a twenty. "How do I do that?"

"Ask the guy you call Buzz Cut." She pointed at the hotel entrance. "Look, he's right inside the lobby door."

Chapter Fifty-seven

Sever dodged the doorman and pushed through the rotating doors. Stumbling over a piece of someone's luggage, he watched Buzz Cut enter the elevator. Sever sprinted toward him as the elevator doors slowly closed, and the man stared straight ahead, never looking at him. Too late he reached the elevator, punching the button, but the car was on its way up.

The first-floor number lit up and paused.

The second-floor number lit up and paused.

The third-floor number lit up and paused, and Sever turned away in defeat and disgust. Maybe the guy *was* staying at the hotel. Regardless, it was clear that Buzz Cut was watching every move that he and Ginny made.

"It can't be Beau." Ginny came up behind him.

"He's involved. Somehow, he's involved."

Walking into his room, he ignored the message light, stripped off the hospital shirt and the rest of his clothes, and hit the shower. There was dried blood on his chest and he checked to make sure he wasn't wounded somewhere. He didn't have a scratch, and Jamie's blood washed down the drain. He towel dried and pulled on a clean pair of jeans and a T-shirt.

Ginny had elected to go back to her room and see if she could arrange his hospital interview with Chilli. Sever poured himself a shot of Dewars and added a splash of water. Pulling out his laptop, he typed in the events in the park. The one thing that came back to him was the motorcycle. The last thing he remembered before Charlie White was shot in his limo was a motorcycle pulling out around the car.

Chapter Fifty-eight

He punched in the code. Three messages.

"Mr. Sever. This is the front desk. We double-checked and Mr. Beaureguard did not leave a forwarding message."

Sever drained the Scotch and poured himself another. If there was an excuse for getting drunk, getting shot at was at the top of the list.

The second message was silence. About ten seconds of silence, and he could hear someone breathing on the line. Very faintly, someone was breathing. He replayed the message then discarded it.

He imagined a more relaxed moment in his life, a time when gunshots and burning buildings weren't in his future. When this life as an entertainment journalist had been fun and rewarding. He sipped the Scotch and thought of a night in Miami—a Paul Simon concert. He and Simon, sitting on the edge of the stage before the show, legs dangling over the edge. Talking about life . . . *the* life. Simon had been more expressive with his songs than with his verbal expressions. Without a break in the conversation he had started strumming his guitar and singing, as if the song would express the sheer frustration of real life more than just words alone.

"I met my old lover on the street last night . . ."

Sever had thought many times about the refrain. "Still crazy, after all these years."

Maybe that was what was wrong with him. He was crazy, and Ginny seemed to be the only one who knew it.

The third message was a friendly female voice.

"Mick. You can see Chilli tomorrow, 10 A.M. Do you want me to come along? If you don't, I can do some more checking on Charlie White and try to find out where T-Beau is. Let me know."

He decided to hang it up for the night. Another Scotch and he'd be no good to anyone, so he may as well just chill out on his own. He thought about calling Ginny, but it might not be a good idea to push a good thing.

The phone startled him. He grabbed the receiver.

"Mick?"

The voice sounded familiar. Not Beau, not Nick, not Chilli or Jamie. "Joseph?"

"Hey. I heard you had a rough time in the park."

"And how did you hear that?"

"Oh, I've got my sources. Listen, Mick, I don't understand why you feel you have to pursue this case anymore. I think that Nick will be all right. No one can prove that he had a connection to the killing. And I believe with all my heart that Chilli D will be found guilty, so—"

Sever interrupted. "The question is, Joseph," he said, stressing the name, "do you believe Chilli *is* guilty?"

"Doesn't make much of a difference. He had the gun and the motive, didn't he?"

"And your impression is that he deserves to pay for past and present transgressions, even if he didn't commit this crime."

"You said that, Mick. I didn't."

"Reverend"—Joseph didn't correct him this time—"why did you call?"

"Mick, my sister is very distressed over her son being in prison, and over you attacking her family. She asked for your help, not your harassment. I'm asking you to please, drop this investigation or whatever it is you're doing."

"Joseph, are you aware that there is a rumor that your brother-in-law had an affair with Margarite Haller?"

No answer.

"Joseph?"

"I assumed you'd come back from Barbados with that story. The nanny, Phillip Teese, is, well, he's not quite all together. He's getting on in years, his wife has a condition, and, Mick, he doesn't remember everything the way it happened."

"You're saying it didn't happen?"

"I'm saying you'd better have proof if you're going to run that story. That's all. I don't want anyone else getting hurt, and obviously that story could hurt Alicia and Amber very much."

"I'm a professional, Reverend. If I run a story I have the facts, alright?"

"Mick, I'm not suggesting anything to the contrary."

The alcohol robbed his inhibitions. Ginny had told him before that, given the right set of circumstances, he could be a nasty drunk.

"I'm sorry, Reverend. In the last few days I've been in the middle of a firebombing, I've been followed all over the city, and I've been in someone's crosshairs. I'm a little punchy."

"Mick, I'm sorry. I did call to ask you to focus your attention on Chilli D. I believe he is my brother-in-law's killer, and I want to see him pay the penalty."

"Is that a Christian attitude?"

"I do believe in this case that the end justifies the means. An example can be made of what comes of violent lyrics and lifestyles."

"I'll come to my own conclusion." He drained his Scotch.

"Mick, I pray for your safety. I pray that if you continue your investigation and encounter more difficulties, the Lord will deliver a gathering of angels to protect you."

"Maybe He already has, Reverend. I'm still standing."

Chapter Fifty-nine

Fuckin' wid da man in blue, you mind-fuck him he mind-fuck you.

Hey, Five O, take this piece of steel, stick it in you, hear you squeal.

Like when I stick my little ho, stick her hard and stick her low.

Sever ejected Chilli's CD and shivered. Hard to defend, until you realized that he'd experienced the cops firsthand. The story was that when he was arrested for his first murder, two arresting officers worked him over pretty good. They claimed he'd pulled a knife. Chilli D claimed they kicked him around for half an hour, then planted the knife on him. So maybe you wrote what you knew. Maybe it was alright to harbor fantasies of revenge. For some people life was a bitch. And then you die.

In the music he could hear the cry of the ghetto kid who wanted to be a player, hanging on the corner, selling the crack, pushing the pussy, playing a role that made him the man of the moment. And then there were the ghetto girls, players in their own right like Lil' Kim and even J. Lo. Ghetto girls who could hold their own with the boys.

Rapper Amie Joe had layed it out for him in an interview several years before. She'd talked about the players. "The player be a tough guy, be a smooth operator. He got respect for holdin' his own. He does it his way. Not the pretender, but the real player. A player who do it his way, he maybe got a wife, his girlfriend," she hung on to the *rl* and dropped the *d*, like "girrrrrlllllfrin'," rough but sexy, "and he got his mistress and he be a player when he sit 'em down and make 'em each understand their role, you know what I'm sayin'?" Then she'd waved her hand. "Now the woman player, she understand that man, but she got nothin' to do with it. She just walk away and get her own game goin'."

Sever remembered the interview well. Ginny pinned him with it the day it came out.

"Could she have described you any more accurately? You are the perfect example of a player, Mick, but I'm not going to play the role you want me to, and I'm not going to get involved in your game. I'll get my own game goin', thank you."

It was shortly thereafter that she walked out the door.

Maybe all writers spoke from their heart and spoke what they knew was true, no matter how offensive it may sound to others. Maybe all writers were players, no matter how it influenced others.

Sever lay back on the bed, hands folded behind his head. Staring at the ceiling, he saw the beginnings of a crack, starting by the door and moving to the center of the room. He remembered the James Taylor lyrics about restless souls and lost love. "Road maps in a well-cracked ceiling, the signs aren't hard to find." There were no signs anywhere. If life was only as easy as road maps in a well-cracked ceiling. If this story was only as easy to follow. At least those cracks led to somewhere.

He stood up, walked to the desk, and flipped on his laptop, gazing at the gray screen as it flickered to life. Writing about an attempt on *his* life was one thing, but explaining the consequences of that attempt was much more difficult. His actions had caused other people to be hurt. And he wondered about the rappers. How did a Chilli D feel when his words caused someone else to be hurt? When another ghetto kid decided to knife a cop because Chilli had said it was okay in his song.

He felt the pain in his shoulder, that reminder of the Barbados incident, and he massaged his throbbing knee, the reminder of his own stupidity. He'd been hurt by his own actions before, but this time he almost got someone else killed.

He stared at the screen and it stared back at him—no answers. No road maps. He'd have to find them himself. Very, very soon, or someone else may die.

Chapter Sixty

The police officer led him down the polished tiled hallway to Chilli's room. An armed officer sat outside on a hardback wooden chair, leafing through a copy of *Vogue* magazine. She raised her eyebrows as they approached, said nothing but stood and opened the door. Sever noticed her holster was unsnapped. Inside, another officer lounged in a vinyl upholstered chair and Chilli D sat up in bed, a loose-fitting hospital gown hanging limply on his shoulders and arms, his neck swathed in bandages. He smiled when he saw Sever.

"Where's Beau?" he croaked. The voice was rough and raspy. Sever could see the strain on his face when he tried to talk.

"I don't know where he is. But I need to ask you some questions. Chilli, you told me the congressman was on your case. You said he was threatening to stop any comeback chances you might have had. You told me that you and Nick had a conversation about how much better things would be without the congressman."

Chilli looked at him without expression.

"Man, everything points to you. Everything."

"Man, we been through this before. I know it looks bad, but I didn't shoot him." He sounded like a drunken reveler at a Chicago Bears game in Soldiers Field, hoarse and straining to be heard.

"Who did? Nick?"

"Could have been. In his office he and his stepdaddy did everything but two-step that day he came in. Scream at each other, 'bout to whip each other's ass."

"It got a little loud?"

"Nicky sayin', 'You made a lot of money off the music business, and this shit never bothered you before.' And Shapply sayin', 'A man can change.' Nicky looks at him cold and says, 'You never gonna change. You're a bottom-feeding crook, and that's never gonna change.' Nick said, 'I'll kill you, old man. You fuck with me, I'll kill you.' "

"Jesus." The two officers were paying rapt attention. "He really threatened Shapply?"

"He did that."

"Chilli, why did you try to kill yourself?" Straight and to the point. Sever glanced at the officers, both sitting in chairs in opposite corners of the room. They had no intention of leaving. There would be no privacy.

Chilli motioned to the second bed. "Sit down. We got things to discuss."

"Things?"

"The congressman had it out for me. There was no way I was gonna get another record contract when he was through with those hearings. He made it clear to Nick and me. Wanted to use me as an example, he said. I flew to Washington that day, but I didn't kill him. Nicky and me, we talked about what it would be like with him out of the way, but I been set up, man. Set up."

"Who?"

"Whoever tried to kill me."

"So it wasn't a suicide attempt?"

"Hell, I got too many responsibilities to die, you know what I'm sayin'? There's five women depend on Chill for everything. I got expenses, man. I'm not about hangin' myself."

"What happened?" Sever sensed the interest from the police officers.

"I'm out for exercise. When I get back to the cage, they were ready for me. One guy holds me and the other puts the rope around my neck. And everybody try to say it's suicide. My ass!" He coughed, hacking into a tissue he took from the nightstand beside his bed. "Guard cut me down just in time."

"Who set you up? Nick?"

"Nah. I thought about it. I owe the man money. I can't pay it back if I'm in jail. Besides, he's in the slammer, too. Still . . ."

"Did you tell someone that the money you owed Nick would be forgiven if you killed Robert Shapply?"

"Hell, no. Who's gonna pay $250,000 to have someone killed. Shit, you hire a guy for fifty bucks and a daily fix to do that work. Man would be a fool to pay that kind of money." He paused. " 'Course, the rumor is that Notorious BIG paid a cool mill for the Crips to hit Tupac. But if that's true, he *was* a fool."

"Once again, who set you up? Who tried to have you killed?"

"Somebody planted the gun in my home. Lots of people know where I live. Breakin' in to anybody's crib is simple. I used to do it sometimes, you know, before I . . ." He hesitated.

"And?"

"Could've been anybody."

"Who did you piss off the most?"

"Everybody I come in contact with. I piss 'em all off."

"Chilli, think. Who would want you set up for the murder of Robert Shapply?"

"Only one that makes any sense. Only one I can tie it to."

"Nick?"

"It's all I can think of. Hated the old man, and had nothing to lose."

"I don't want to believe that."

"You still want to believe I killed him. Shit, it's easy pick-ins. The black guy with the rap sheet." Chilli got a pained look on his face. "I'll tell you who didn't set me up. None of the five bitches. Shit, they depend on me. Chill goes down, they all got to go find work."

Chapter Sixty-one

The sun warmed the slightly chilled air, and the comfortable temperature was perfect for shirtsleeves. He had the cab stop several blocks before, and he walked back to the hotel.

"Mr. Sever . . ." The bellman intercepted him. "There's a lady who's been asking for you. She's . . ." He looked toward the desk. "She's not there. Must have taken off. She waited about half an hour." He shrugged his shoulders.

"What did she look like?"

"Sam talked to her. I just saw her from a distance. Maybe she's in the restroom. I just thought you ought to know."

Sever studied the lobby. Three people stood at the desk, two checking in and one arguing over her bill. Two women sat on a leather couch speaking in a foreign language and waving their hands. No one looked familiar. He wondered if Alicia Shapply would make a move here in the hotel. It couldn't be her.

Sever stepped into the gift shop just off the desk. There was no one except the clerk, who nodded and went back to reading her Sue Grafton paperback. He positioned himself behind a kiosk of sunglasses, warily watching the lobby activity through the glass window.

She emerged from the lobby restroom, looking in both directions. Proceeding to the desk she engaged the available clerk, who reached down and handed her a well-worn travel bag. Amber Shapply hung it on her shoulder and started toward the doorway.

"You're a long way from home." Sever stepped forward and tapped her on the shoulder. She spun around and he saw raw fear in her eyes.

"Mick."

"Hey, settle down. You came all this way to see me?"

"You, and Nick."

"And your mother?"

"Oh, hell. You know?"

"Know what?" Sever motioned to a seat.

"No. Not here. Let's walk. Anywhere." She was scared.

"Okay." He pushed open the door and they emerged, facing the busy street. She glanced furtively up and down the sidewalk, put her head down as if charging a bull, and started walking. Sever hurried to catch up.

"So talk."

She set the pace, dressed in a pair of faded blue jeans, a weathered leather jacket, and a pair of dirty white Nikes.

"Is anyone following us?"

"No. Maybe." Too damned many people following other people. He glanced behind them. "Amber, what is this all about?"

She turned abruptly and darted into a small sandwich shop. Sever followed. He caught up with her and grabbed her shoulder. "Amber, what the hell is this all about?"

She scooted into the booth at the rear of the shop. She spoke softly. "Mick. She called me." Amber glanced over her shoulder out the plate glass window.

"Your mother?"

"Yes."

"And?"

"She threatened Margarite and me."

"For what? Something about contesting the will again?"

"No. I told you. This never had anything to do with the will."

"Then what?"

"You know what. I think I know who killed Margarite Haller."

Sever was quiet, watching her expression. She couldn't look him in the eye; her gaze was centered on the table in front of her.

"I think my father killed her."

"So why didn't you tell me this from the beginning?"

"I needed someone else to believe it, too."

"I believe your father may have had a fling with the girl, but there's no proof. An affair, Amber. Murder's a pretty serious accusation."

"Serious? It may have gotten him killed."

"Slow down. Start from the beginning. You know you're getting into some pretty deep shit here."

She laughed out loud. "Oh, it may get deeper than you can imagine. Mick, let me face the door." She stood up and waited for him to move.

"Amber?"

"I was very young and after all, it was my father, for Christ's sake. Why would I even dream he was fucking her? She flaunted herself, Mick. Even at thirteen, and she *was* thirteen, she knew what she had. I think back now and wonder about her father. Did he have something to do with it? Did he molest her?"

"Amber, this isn't necessarily a good thing to talk about."

"Oh, shit! You're going to give me a lesson in morality? Little girls throwing themselves at rock stars. At you, and my brother. How many entertainers are fucking underage girls right now?" She paused, squinting her eyes, looking past him to the window.

"All right, what made you—"

"So she's telling me how cute my father is. How attentive my father is. How giving my father is. And I'm just happy she's having a good time on the island. He's calling us 'his girls,' and buying us stuff. Then he buys her this bikini."

"A bikini?"

"Yeah."

"And your mother?"

"She's not paying any attention at all. She's shopping, she's on the phone to her friends back home. To be honest, I can't even remember her being around back then. Just my father."

"And what did he buy you?"

"Squat. I didn't have a figure. He has me give her the bikini, and it's the first time I ever realized she really had a serious frame. I didn't." She looked down past her chest to her legs. "Still don't."

"A bikini doesn't mean anything happened."

"Will you just shut up and listen?"

A tired-looking waitress in an ill-fitting uniform wandered over to the booth, flipped an oversprayed wave of hair out of her face, and pulled a frayed order pad from her apron. "What'll it be?"

"Two black," Amber said. She waited till the waitress retreated. "So, she's got these great little tits and she puts on this white bikini, telling me how all the boys want to touch her tits. I've got none. She puts on the bottom half and her round butt is hanging out, and she tells me that the boys want to feel it."

The waitress sat the pot on the table. "Anything else?"

Amber dismissed her with a wave. "Then she parades around my father, her chest sticking out—and her ass—and my father complimenting her, telling her she was going to be a real looker someday. I'm thinking, *someday?*"

"Amber, a guy can be attracted to younger girls. That doesn't make him a pedophile."

She frowned. "So I've thought about it. Reconstructed things over the years. She'd go back in the afternoon for naps and I'd stay by the pool. Or he'd suggest we visit the studio and listen to the band rehearse. He knew I wanted my beach time but she'd go with him. In that little white bikini. They'd come back a couple of hours later, and even though it's probably my latter-day imagination after this many years, I think I knew that something was wrong."

"So you've built this case in your mind?"

"Final piece of the puzzle." She grabbed his hand and held on for dear life. "This is not something I dreamed up in the last twenty-some years. Margarite and I are in bed one night, lying next to each other, and she leans over and says, 'Have you ever fucked before?' And me, I'm not even sure what all's involved." She shrugged her shoulders. "I said no, and then I asked her the same question. She gives me a big smile and says, 'Yes. Last night on the beach.' "

Sever felt her tremble. "Amber, it proves nothing. Nothing." He freed his hand and poured the two of them a cup of coffee. He found his hand shaking, as if he'd picked up her vibrations. "Where's your daughter?"

"I can't tell you. She's safe. I pray she's safe, Mick." She glanced at the window once more. "I think I knew then. It all went together. And then she was with him the night of the picnic." Her voice was now steady, cold, and her eyes pierced his. "He left and five minutes later she did, too. I never told anyone, and I never saw her again." Her face broke, tears watering her cheeks, and when she started sobbing he moved to her side of the booth. The congressman's daughter buried her face in Sever's shoulder and cried.

Chapter Sixty-two

She huddled in an almost fetal position on the bed, head bent, eyes peering up at Sever. She'd thrown her coat and bag on the floor, and kicked off her running shoes, giving all the appearances of a homeless waif.

"Tell Ginny what you told me." Sever straddled the desk chair. All of a sudden his hotel room felt a lot smaller.

"I called an attorney I know. Don Witter. He was a friend years ago, and I thought maybe he could give me some advice."

Ginny leaned forward in the lounge chair, hands folded in front of her. "How was he a friend?"

"He'd been a friend of the family."

"First mistake," Sever said.

"God. I wasn't thinking. I just knew that I had to talk to someone. Don had helped me out a couple of times when I had some problems, so it was just natural."

"So you told him you felt certain your father was having

an affair with your friend Margarite twenty years ago in Barbados, and he called your mother?"

"He called her."

"And maybe your father?"

"If he called my mother, I'm sure he called my father as well."

"Time line?" Ginny looked back and forth at Sever and Amber.

"I'm sorry?" Amber appeared confused.

"When did you call the attorney?"

"Three days before my father was killed. And I didn't just suggest an affair. I suggested that I thought my father may have killed Margarite and asked him what I should do."

"Jesus! What did you expect to happen?"

Amber's temper flared. "Who the hell was I supposed to go to? The Barbados police? I knew that they'd been paid off for years. I needed legal advice. Isn't that what attorneys are supposed to give?"

Sever reached back and picked up his Scotch. "Apparently not this attorney."

Ginny guided the conversation back on track. "So your father is killed. Chilli D is arrested, your brother is arrested, and you have no contact with the family. . . ."

"Except for Nick. I was able to talk to him."

"You have no contact with your mother, and then out of the blue she calls and threatens you?"

"Do you know that the governor of Florida is about to appoint her to the United States Congress? She's going to finish out my father's term. And I'm still certain that my father is a murderer."

"What did she say?"

"She said to drop it. She said that there have been other people who have died because of my suggestion, and it had to stop."

Ginny stood up and looked down on the girl. "What was the threat?"

"She said if I pursued my accusation, there might be another Margarite who meets an untimely end, and even though she didn't want that to happen, there was nothing she would be able to do about it."

"No!"

"I swear to Christ."

Sever threw back a swallow of Scotch. "And I thought my family was fucked-up."

Chapter Sixty-three

Jamie Jordan was sitting up, his chest, shoulder, and arm wrapped in a castlike material.

"Jamie, it's got to be tough." Sever pointed at the cast. "That's your smoking arm."

"Man, you talk about quitting cold turkey. Haven't had one yet, Mick. Might be a good time to quit."

"So you're feeling better?"

"I am. The paper is paying me extra for hazardous duty."

"A lot of things are coming together. I think we've got another reason why someone may have killed the congressman."

"Besides the hearings?"

Sever sat down on the hard wooden chair. "Jamie, we're close. I don't think Chilli shot him."

"Who did?"

"I think that the congressman had an affair with a thirteen-year-old girl in Barbados. And just when he's about to hold these hearings about the immorality of rock and roll, someone threatened to expose him."

"You're serious?" Jamie was practically salivating.

"As a heart attack."

"Who shot him?"

"There were probably only three or four people who knew. One was Bobby Jergan, Shapply's business partner in Barbados. I think he knew, and somebody killed him. I think Alicia Shapply knows, and her daughter Amber knows."

Jamie was hanging on every word. "Damn. This is going to be a better story than we ever imagined. Hell, this should be in the *National Enquirer*, Mick."

"Somebody killed the little girl in Barbados, and my guess is that it's the congressman. Maybe he was afraid she'd tell someone. Maybe she did."

"Why do I get the feeling that there's a big 'but' coming?"

"But we can't prove any of this. Hell, Jamie, it took place twenty years ago. No evidence, no DNA matches back then . . ."

"So someone shot the congressman because the accusation of his affair would put a screeching halt to the hearings."

"I believe that's a strong possibility."

"Mick, we can go with that. You can always write the story from a 'is there a chance' perspective. Is there a chance that this happened? Is there a chance that Chilli D is not guilty?"

"I won't do it, Jamie. I want to prove that Chilli and Nick Brand are clean."

Chapter Sixty-four

He called the hotel from the hospital lobby and asked for his voice-mail messages. They patched him through.

"Mick." The voice was flat, dead. "You need to meet me." Ginny sounded tired, almost drugged. She gave him an address downtown, southeast. Sever wasn't that familiar with Washington, but he knew this wasn't the nicest section of the city. "I've got some information about Alicia Shapply and Chilli. Please, Mick. As soon as possible."

She needed to get back to Chicago, or take a long trip with him to the Keys. The latter sounded better.

Sever approached the taxi parked outside. He gave him the address.

"Are you sure, man?"

Sever thought for a second. If it was a setup, if the Ice Maiden was going to make another attempt on his life, he got the feeling this was the place to do it.

"Yeah. I'm meeting a good friend. She gave me this address."

"Hey, keep the doors locked, and you pay me before I let you out."

He thought for a fleeting second. This wasn't part of the plan. Whatever happened to sex, drugs, and rock and roll? *This* sounded seriously dangerous. But it was Ginny. Ginny. He climbed into the backseat. Sever glanced back at the hospital as the taxi pulled away from the curb. He could swear that Buzz Cut was standing by the entrance, with the collar up on his trench coat.

Chapter Sixty-five

The driver took a well-chosen route through the city, ending up in a decrepit neighborhood with ramshackle houses, boarded-up businesses, and overgrown vacant lots with weeds choking the outcrop of brick and mortar that once had been a thriving community. Sever looked out the windows, watching the occasional child peek from behind a building. Other than that, the neighborhood looked deserted.

"Hey, man, you sure this is where you supposed to be?" The cab driver had both hands on the wheel, his grip getting tighter the closer they got.

He pulled up in front of an old brick church, its cold gray concrete porch cracked and crumbling. Large chunks of the steps were missing, and the brick was almost black from years of pollution and neglect. Boards covered the large window frames where it appeared that stained-glass panes may have been displayed. A rusted Volkswagen Beetle sat up on concrete blocks on the ground, the windows busted out of it and the original color just a faded memory.

Sever gazed up at the steeple, leaning dangerously to the right.

"Pay me now, man, and make it quick."

He handed the driver the money plus a twenty-dollar tip, then cautiously stepped out.

Climbing up the steps, he stepped over a collection of empty wine bottles that cluttered the doorway. The smell of urine was strong as he pushed on the scarred wooden door and it groaned on rusted hinges. Sever walked into the entranceway, a dim light coming through the cracks in the boarded-up windows lighting his way.

He stumbled, bumping a large object that was propped against the wall. Stepping back, he studied it for a moment. A Harley Davidson. In his head he could hear the throaty roar as the bike left the park. Harley Davidson had patented their sound. No other bike could sound like a Harley. He'd remember that sound as long as he was alive. T-Beau rode a Harley. And so did Chilli.

He reached the sanctuary where light filtered in from holes in the ceiling. He could make out only three rows of seats in the large empty room, and somewhere up above a bird fluttered. He stopped.

"Ginny?"

The bird beat the air. There was no other sound.

"Ginny!"

"Over here." It wasn't Ginny's voice.

Sever's eyes grew accustomed to the dim light. Ginny and Amber were seated side by side.

"Ginny?"

There was no answer.

He stepped closer and saw that duct tape had sealed their mouths shut. Both ladies had their hands behind their back, and Ginny's eyes grew wide when she saw him. Sever knew instinctively that she'd put up one hell of a fight. Amber's head hung low, and she never looked up.

"Sit down." That voice. The voice from late-night television, the resonant tones. Joseph Evans stepped out of the darkness, produced a black pistol, and aimed it at Sever's midsection. Sever sat down.

"Mick, it's just gone too far. You just don't know when to say *when*, do you?"

Sever looked up at the man, trying to make out all of his features in the dim light. He wanted to describe this as accurately as possible when he wrote the story.

"Time after time we tried to get you to back off. You wouldn't pay attention. Now look. You've put your ex-wife in jeopardy, my niece in jeopardy—why didn't you just walk away?"

"I suppose now would be too late."

Evans ignored him. "You've spent a lot of time and effort trying to get to the bottom of this, haven't you?" The voice was condescending. "And this is what it all comes down to."

"What? That you're going to kill us?"

"Mick, I told you before, I believe that the end justifies the means. In a war, soldiers die. But at the end of that war, there is peace. Soldiers die to make this world a better place."

"Just like that? You don't think someone is going to figure this out?"

"This is downtown Southeast, a nasty part of town. Washington, D.C., is the murder capital of the world. Not a good combination, Mick. And you're famous for sticking your nose in places it doesn't belong. So if someone were to find your body in a boarded-up house in two or three weeks, it will probably go down as another unsolved D.C. murder." He let down his arm, the pistol pointing at the floor. Sever saw him glance at the ceiling where the bird was flapping its wings, swooping up and down, apparently not happy about being disturbed.

Sever leaped at him, springing with surprising strength and agility. His knee stayed strong as he hit Evans chest level, landing on top of him as he knocked the man on his back. He rolled off and struggled to stand, pushing with his arms, his bruised shoulder screaming with pain as he fell back to the floor. He felt the kick to his ribs and rolled to avoid another. Evans was up, kicking him again, this time in the groin, and he grabbed himself with both hands and willed himself not to heave on the floor.

"Mick, I'll kill you now. And then I'll kill the girls. Now get back on that bench."

Sever struggled to the pew, his rib cage, knee, shoulder, and groin all aching. Ginny's eyes were closed as if she couldn't bear to see him in this agony.

Evans held the gun level, waiting for another attack. "There's a big picture here that you can't possibly understand. Our society has become permissive on such a scale as to threaten the entire future of mankind. Can you understand that?" He seemed to wait for an answer as the bird beat the air above him. "The entire future of mankind. And you, Mr. Sever, as you glamorize the music industry, are largely responsible."

"And you're going to make things right?" Sever's voice was weak, the energy drained from his body.

"We have allowed immoral people to have loud voices and celebrity status. It is time to take back the morality issue. There are no shades of gray, Mick. There is black, and there is white."

"And what was Robert Shapply? Black or white?"

"Black. As the ace of spades. You see, as Amber has correctly assumed, Robert Shapply did in fact have an affair with a young teenage girl. That affair resulted in a young girl's loss of innocence. That affair resulted in a young girl's murder. And that affair resulted in the death of the congressman."

Amber Shapply quietly sobbed, her crying muffled by the tape over her mouth.

"One evil act, and look at the consequences."

"Did you kill Robert Shapply?"

"Someone had to. The good that could have been accomplished by the man, the hearings on pornography and violence in today's world of entertainment, all that was about to be compromised."

"Compromised?"

"Amber was about to accuse her father of having an affair with Margarite Haller. And the congressman had decided to admit to the affair. He actually believed that people would forgive him. No. His crisis of conscience would have ruined everything we had worked for. Our cause would have been destroyed."

"You killed Robert Shapply? If Amber was going to accuse him, why didn't you kill *her*?

"She was blood, Mick. I was hoping I wouldn't have to go

there. I prayed that she would drop the matter."

"And you killed Charlie White."

Evans bowed his head for just a second. "Charlie was a good man, but a soldier in the war nonetheless."

"And you tried to kill me. In the park, on the bike."

"We wouldn't be here today if I'd been successful."

"Jesus, you're a one-man wrecking crew."

"We couldn't seem to get rid of you." His voice rose and trembled. "All you had to do was go away. The police were happy with Chilli's guilt."

"And the congressman killed Margarite Haller so she wouldn't tell anyone?"

Evans sighed. "It's regrettable you won't get to write the ending to this story." He motioned with his pistol. "I want the three of you to get up and walk to the rear of the sanctuary. There's a small study off to the right."

"One more question. Did you think that making it look like Chilli committed suicide would solve everything? Prove his guilt? You ran out of luck on that one, too, didn't you?"

The Reverend smiled with that condescending look on his face.

Slowly easing himself up, Sever watched the man, his arm steady as he pointed his weapon. He reached down and took Ginny by the elbow, helping her to her feet. Then he helped Amber. The three of them stood, waiting to be escorted to the study. Ginny's eyes were red, rimmed with tears, but even in the gloom he saw determination. Determination didn't mean squat when the man had a gun. Lambs to the slaughter.

The squeaking of the rusty hinges echoed through the sanctuary as someone opened the door and entered the narthex. They froze as silence returned. Even the frenetic flapping of the bird ceased. Sever listened carefully. The door had opened, but had not closed. Now there was just silence. Then sharp, staccato steps clicked on the floor as the intruder worked his way back to the sanctuary.

"What a cozy reunion." Alicia Shapply stood in the doorway, her shadow blocking the little light that shown through. "I can't see that well, but I'm assuming that my daughter, Mr. Sever, and the former Mrs. Sever are all present?"

"Alicia. You probably shouldn't be here."

"Oh, Joseph. I should be here. This is an end and a beginning. It's not often one gets to be a part of both."

"Mrs. Shapply." Sever could make out her severe features. A dress, heels, her hair recently styled. She was definitely out of place. "You hired someone to firebomb the studio in Barbados?"

"Is this the time for confessions, Mr. Sever? Is this where I boldly tell you how I've masterminded this charade?"

Sever walked toward her.

"That's far enough, Mick!" Evans stood behind him, and Sever stopped.

"No, Mrs. Shapply, this is where we tell you that we know your second husband had an affair with a thirteen-year-old girl. What's the problem, Mrs. S.? Weren't you enough for him? He had to get what he needed from a thirteen-year-old?"

She bristled. "He was a sick man. Do you understand that? A sick man!" She controlled herself. "I've lived with that for twenty years. For twenty years I've avoided his touch. It had nothing to do with me, Mr. Sever. It had everything to do with a loose little girl and a very sick man."

They were all watching and listening, and as long as someone was talking, they were still all alive. Sever pushed harder.

"But he's dead. Your brother killed him. Did you see to that?"

"Alicia . . ." Evans tried to get her attention, but she was on a roll.

"See to it? Was it my idea? Yes. The sick man was about to tell the world of his affair, because my lovely daughter, after twenty years, decided to go public with her childhood memory. We couldn't let that happen, Mr. Sever."

"So the sick man paid his price."

"And so did his little girlfriend."

"Did you see to that, too?"

In the dim, fading light he could make out a grim smile on her face. "Yes, I did. I saw to that. When I found them on the beach that night I bashed her head against the rocks. Bashed her head until she stopped breathing. Until the light went out in her eyes. And do you know what my husband did? Zipped up and walked away. We both had a dirty little secret. And they both deserved to die."

He heard Amber screaming in anguish through the duct tape.

"You killed the girl?" He felt flushed, his heart picking up its pace. "You beat her to death on a rock? What the hell kind of an animal are you?"

"Strong words for a man about to die. You see, Mr. Sever, I wasn't about to suffer the consequences of my husband's dalliance. And now, because of you and your incessant snooping, we have to put an end to it all. Enough confessions for one afternoon?" Alicia Shapply folded her hands in front of her.

"Jesus."

"Mr. Sever." Evans pushed the gun into his back. "Please

turn around and escort the ladies to the study. It's time we finished our business."

"Fuck your business, man." The deep, rumbling voice came directly from behind Alicia Shapply. "My man here has a gun in your sister's back. You simply let my people go, Reverend, and I'll make sure your sister lives." T-Beau stepped out from behind the Ice Maiden. Buzz Cut stood to the right with a gun in his hand, pointed at the Ice Maiden.

Sever let out a slow breath. "I didn't think I'd be this happy to see you again, Beau."

"You saved my life. Looks like I can return the favor."

"It's all over, Reverend." Sever reached for the gun.

The pistol exploded in a deafening roar. Sever spun around as the sound echoed through the building. Buzz Cut collapsed on the floor, the pistol falling from his hand and sliding across the floor.

"You're right. It's over. It's perfect, Mick." His voice was syrupy sweet. "Chilli D's bodyguard tried to kill me, and—"

"Chilli D's bodyguard?"

"Who did you think he was?" The Reverend let his gaze go to the fallen man for just a second.

Sever hit him, hard and fast, a quick punch to the stomach, and the man dropped the pistol. Then he caught his jaw, a hard jab that snapped him straight up. The sharp pain in Sever's rib cage was unbearable, but he smashed his fist one last time into the Reverend's face, and Evans's nose went flat, blood spurting from the broken appendage. Evans dropped like a stone.

"Where are those angels now, Reverend?" Sever groaned and fell to the floor. The last thing he heard was T-Beau saying "Call a doctor, man. We got some serious casualties."

Chapter Sixty-six

The music was soft, but he could hear every word. It helped that he'd memorized the lyrics decades ago.

When the moon is high, and you still can't sleep, and she's everywhere you are,
And the clock strikes two, all you can do, is wish upon a star
And still sleep won't come, and it's come undone, and she's coming back no more
It's just you alone and the telephone, as you pace and walk the floor.

"Hey, you awake?"

Sever opened his eyes. It wasn't a nurse this time. "I've been awake for a while. Who put the music on?"

"I don't know. It was on when I walked in." Ginny smiled

down at him. "Cracked ribs, a punctured lung, a broken wrist—you could be worse."

"I could be dead."

"There's that." She pulled up a chair and sat close to the bed.

"Alicia Shapply?"

"The governor apparently isn't going to appoint her to the Congress. They frown on people in jail being appointed to public office."

"What about Buzz Cut? Is there any . . ." He grimaced in pain. The ribs hurt like hell.

"Chilli D had two white bodyguards. Buzz Cut and the guy with the bad complexion."

"What did they possibly want with us?"

"T-Beau says they thought you were out to get Chilli. The first attack was to scare you off."

"Everybody and her *brother* wanted to scare me off."

"Very funny." She crossed her legs, those long beautiful legs in tight denim. "They recognized T-Beau, and he recognized them. So Buzz Cut went up to T-Beau's room after the funeral and apologized for the incident."

"But he kept following you."

"T-Beau told Chilli he should fire the guy who threatened me, but he convinced Buzz Cut to stick around and follow me, and later you. Thank God he did."

Sever tried to sit up, but the pain in his chest was too much. "Why?"

"According to Beau, to protect me. After what happened here and in Barbados he knew you were in some deep shit, and he wanted to make sure I was alright. Personally, I think he wanted to find out what I knew."

"So Beau wasn't involved?"

"No. If Buzz Cut, Daryl, hadn't seen you at the hospital, we might not be having this conversation."

"That was him. So Beau and I are even."

"That's the way he sees it."

"Daryl?"

"Daryl is going to live. He got shot in the shoulder but he's going to be fine. Buzz Cut will survive."

"I thought Beau was mixed up in it."

"When he moved out of the hotel I thought you might be right. He said he had to get away from the action for a while, and being around the two of us was being in the thick of it."

"Chilli?"

"Joseph planted the gun in his apartment. They've let Chilli go."

"Amber must be—"

"Devastated. Other than her daughter and the short-order cook, she's go no one."

"She's got her brother."

"Yeah. He's out. Wants to know if you're up for a trip to Graceland?"

"I'm not up for that. I think he and I need to leave things where they are. What about you?"

"And Nick? It's in the past, Sever."

"A lot of things are."

"You and I need to leave things where they are."

"Probably. Although it was a nice break."

"You know, Mick, the older I get the more confusing relationships get."

"They should get easier."

"They don't."

T-Beau continued to sing the sad love lament.

It's just you alone and the telephone, as you pace and walk the floor.

"Where's Beau?"

"He said he's thinking of you and he flew back to L.A."

"And Jamie?"

"Down the hall. He's so excited you two are here together."

"Oh, God!"

"I'm flying out this afternoon. You going to be okay?"

"I'm fine. I do better by myself. Unless," he said, pausing, "unless I'm with you. You bring out the best in me. You know that."

"Oh, hell. It's the morphine or whatever they're giving you. Make sure you spell my name right in the book, Mick."

"When the Reverend and Alicia go on trial, do you want to be here?"

"I've got some business in Chicago. Let me see how that goes, and I'll let you know."

She leaned down and kissed him on the lips. Then she was gone.

It's just you alone and the telephone, as you pace and walk the floor.